Jo's intuition screamed

She pictured herself hurling
through the window. But her body didn't carry
out the command.

There was no noise from the box. No odor. No
change in temperature. No flashing lights. No
electrical discharge. No explosion. But she felt
as if an explosion had gone off inside her head.
Somehow she *knew* that the box was the source
of the sudden, terrible pain.

Get away, her brain screamed. With
superhuman effort, Jo stood up. Her legs were
no stronger than flower stems. Before she could
take a step, her knees buckled and she collapsed
to the floor. As the box bounced beside her,
shock waves reverberated in her head. She tried
to scream; no sound came out.

Get away! Arms and legs wouldn't obey her
commands. She lay on her side, helpless,
disoriented, a prisoner in her own body—and
more terrified than she'd ever been in her life.

Dear Reader,

We're delighted to bring you the second book in Rebecca York's exciting ongoing series for Harlequin Intrigue, 43 LIGHT STREET.

It looks like a charming old building near the renovated Baltimore waterfront, but inside 43 Light Street lurks danger...and romance.

As you found with #143 *Life Line,* the book that introduced the series, and you will find with *Shattered Vows* and all the future 43 LIGHT STREET books, Rebecca York spins spine-tingling thrillers, eerie psychological suspense and good ol' adventure stories—all laced with the passion and romance that you expect from Harlequin.

Rebecca York is the pseudonym of two Maryland writers—Ruth Glick and Eileen Buckholtz. Longtime lovers of romance and mystery, they have penned mainstream psychological thrillers as Samantha Chase, a young-adult mystery series under their real names, romances as Amanda Lee, and of course, an award-winning suspense series, Peregrine Connection, as Rebecca York.

We hope you're enjoying this and all the upcoming titles in their newest series—43 LIGHT STREET. Be sure to look for the 43 LIGHT STREET logo to identify future books.

Sincerely,

Debra Matteucci
Senior Editor and Editorial Coordinator

Shattered Vows

Vows

Rebecca York

Harlequin Books

TORONTO • NEW YORK • LONDON
AMSTERDAM • PARIS • SYDNEY • HAMBURG
STOCKHOLM • ATHENS • TOKYO • MILAN

We appreciate the assistance of
Mary Kilchenstein,
for her help with the Baltimore locale;
Neal Sipe, Band Director of
Towson High School,
for providing the lyrics to the school song;
and Dr. DeAnne Byerly,
Baltimore County Criminal Justice Coordinator,
for advice about legal procedures.

To Debra Matteucci,
who can hang out her shingle at
43 Light Street anytime

Harlequin Intrigue edition published February 1991

ISBN 0-373-22155-X

SHATTERED VOWS

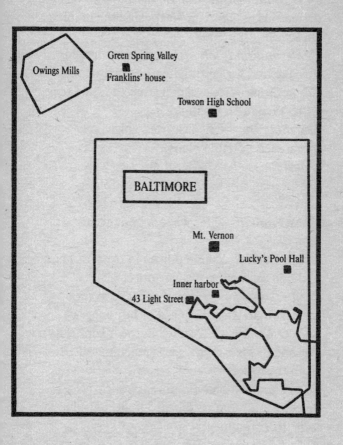

Owings Mills

Green Spring Valley

Franklins' house

Towson High School

BALTIMORE

Mt. Vernon

Lucky's Pool Hall

Inner harbor

43 Light Street

CAST OF CHARACTERS

Jo O'Malley—She took on her most dangerous assignment—exposing the maniac who was stalking her.

Cameron Randolph—This inventor had his own agenda for getting involved with Jo.

Eddie Cahill—He escaped from the state pen with revenge on his mind.

Laughing Boy—His distorted voice threatened horrible plans.

Laura Roswell—Her legal practice was prospering, but her marriage was falling apart.

Abby Franklin—Her wedding put Jo in danger.

Collin Randolph—He'd been in over his head and had seen only one way out.

Steve Claiborne—Was it a mistake to fix up his best man with the maid of honor?

Skip O'Malley—He'd died in the line of duty, but one of his old cases was reaching out from the grave.

Evan Hamill—This Baltimore police detective thought he'd heard it all, until he took Jo's statement.

Chapter One

Eddie Cahill flexed his leg, feeling the reassuring taut-
ness of the knife nestled between his sock and his clammy
flesh. The weapon had cost him plenty, plus a few promised favors once he was on the outside. Which was going
to be in twenty minutes if things kept clicking along according to plan.

In the prison kitchen the weapon had been a harmless
butter spreader. Long, clandestine hours of sharpening
had given it a deadly edge. But the knife was only part of
the elaborate sequence of moves Eddie had been making
since the day they'd locked him up.

His glance strayed from the soap-filled sink where he
was washing pans from dinner. For a fraction of a second he caught Lowery's eye. The man nodded almost
imperceptibly.

The poor geek. In a world where inflicting pain and
suffering was a major recreational activity, Lowery came
in for more than his fair share. But Eddie had seen the
advantage of becoming buddies with a man who suf-
fered from grand mal epileptic seizures. Now he was so
pitifully grateful that he'd do anything for his one friend.

"All right, you bums, finish up so that you can close
the place for the night," a guard barked.

Eddie began to scrub harder. He looked sullenly industrious, but every muscle in his body was tensed for flight. Rinsing the pan, he set it on the drainboard with a noisy clatter.

Behind him Lowery moaned. That was the signal, and Eddie's heart began to pound inside his chest. It was now or never.

A guard started cussing. With everyone else in the room, Eddie turned toward the disturbance. Lowery was already on the floor. His arms and legs jerked violently. His eyes rolled back in his head. His jaw opened and closed. Eddie had seen his fits a couple of times before. Only this evening it was all a put-on.

"Quick. Get somethin' under his tongue," he shouted as he edged toward the door to the garbage room. "'Fore he bites it off."

Nobody looked at Eddie. All eyes were riveted to the man on the floor.

"Jeeze," someone muttered.

Two guards knelt beside Lowery. One held his head; the other inserted the handle of a wooden spoon between his teeth. Eddie didn't stay to watch. In an instant, he was out the door and into the garbage area.

The guard inside whirled at the unauthorized entry. But Eddie was ready for action. Before the guy could unholster his gun or push the alarm buzzer, he plunged the knife into the man's heart. The guard went down with only a gurgle. Eddie took the gun and stuffed the body into the dumpster. Then he climbed in after him and began pulling refuse over both of them.

All the time his ears were tuned for the sound of the garbage truck. If it didn't come on schedule, he'd just iced a man for nothing. Too bad the odds of getting another chance were about a gizillion to one. For several heart-stopping moments, he was sure he'd lost the bet. Then the truck came grinding to a halt.

He waited in the foul-smelling darkness while the dumpster was lifted onto the huge truck. Then the vehicle was rumbling down the service road in back of the kitchen.

He almost blew his supper as he waited for the gate to open. Finally it did. Then the truck was speeding down Route 175. Eddie let out the breath he'd been holding and settled back to wait. He was out. That was the important thing for now. But he had plans. The first thing he was going to do was get even with the women who'd put him in the cooler.

SOCIETY PARTIES weren't exactly her scene, Jo O'Malley thought as she backed her Honda Civic out of the garage and pressed the remote control to close the door. Actually, she conceded with a little laugh, she'd really rather be on a stakeout wearing beat-up clothes with a hat to hide her red hair. Tonight her strawberry-gold ringlets had been coiffed by the Beauty Connection. She'd even sprung for a fifteen-dollar manicure to shape and polish her short nails.

She looked down at the Royal Persian polish, thinking that if Abby Franklin weren't one of her best friends, she would have politely declined the party invitation— except that you could hardly back out of the prewedding festivities when you'd already agreed to be the matron of honor.

As she headed up the Jones Falls Expressway, she turned the radio to her favorite country station, hoping the music would occupy her mind. WPOC was just starting a newscast, and she almost turned the dial. Then the name from a lead story leaped out at her like a ghost from behind a gravestone.

Eddie Cahill.

Jo's foot bounced on the accelerator making the car shoot forward and then slow. Behind her, a truck horn blared, and she struggled to proceed at a steady pace while the newscaster wiped out her sense of security.

"...both Cahill and a guard are missing from the maximum security penitentiary in Jessup, Maryland. Cahill may be armed and is considered extremely dangerous."

Realizing her hands were fused to the wheel, Jo made an effort to unclench her fingers.

Eddie Cahill. She'd thought he was safely behind bars. Now she remembered the terrible scene in the courtroom just after the judge had pronounced sentence. The prisoner had swiveled around, and his glittering black eyes had sliced into her, making it impossible to move. Then he'd fixed his wife and the prosecuting attorney, Jennifer Stark, with the same menacing look. A hush had fallen over the courtroom as every spectator caught the tension.

"No prison can hold me, and when I get out, you three bitches are gonna pay," Eddie had snarled with the voice of a witch doctor delivering a curse.

Jo was rarely spooked, but the absolute confidence of the threat had made her blood run cold. She'd never been so relieved to see a man handcuffed and hustled off to prison.

Now Eddie had made good on the first part of the promise. He'd escaped. Was he going to come after her first? Or was it going to be Jenny or poor Karen?

It had all started when Karen had hired private detective Jo O'Malley to prove that her husband was cheating on her. He'd been cheating, all right. But the infidelity had been like an oil slick floating on top of a polluted river. Eddie had been deep into drug distribution. When the police had closed in on him, the evidence Jo had uncovered had played a crucial role in his conviction.

Jo sucked a shuddering gust of air into her lungs and willed her pulse to slow. She would not let this get to her. Eddie couldn't know where she was. Not so soon. Not tonight. Yet all at once the prospect of spending an evening in the middle of a noisy crowd was very appealing, she realized as she turned in at the long driveway that led to the estate the Franklins used when they weren't at their retirement home in Florida.

Tonight the two-story Moorish-style house was ablaze with lights, and baroque music drifted into the night. Probably there wasn't a parking place near the front door, Jo decided with a sigh, as she pulled into a space near the gate.

She'd assumed her velvet suit would be warm enough. She hadn't counted on a long, cold walk up the tree-lined driveway. Jo folded her arms and hunched her shoulders against the November wind. Above her the remaining leaves on the tall oaks rustled ominously like dried-up decorations left over from Halloween.

A perfect place for an ambush, she reflected with a shiver, as she quickened her step. Someone who wanted to pop out from behind the boxwoods and grab her wouldn't even have to muffle his footsteps.

Her mind clicked back to Eddie Cahill and the evil look on his face that day in court. Only now he was waiting in the inky blackness beyond the circles of light that lined the driveway.

Jo managed a feeble laugh at her overactive imagination. With any luck, the police had already recaptured the man. Escaped criminals didn't stay on the loose for long. She let her mind spin out pictures of roadblocks, squads of uniformed officers on a manhunt, the final capture in a field near the state prison.

"Can I help you, miss?"

The movie in her mind vanished and private detective Josephine O'Malley jumped several inches off the ground. As she came down, she realized she was being addressed by a man in a maroon uniform.

Sheez. He probably thought she was some kind of loony. "I'm here to attend the Franklin-Claiborne party."

He looked around in puzzlement. "Did you arrive by taxi?"

"My car is at the end of the driveway."

"I would have been glad to park it for you, miss."

Jo realized she'd already made her second faux pas in less than a minute. The Franklins had hired parking attendants. But how could you expect a girl from the mountains of western Maryland to know that?

"I'll let you get the car when I leave," she promised as she started up the steps. Moments later she was bathed in the sparkling light of the crystal chandelier that graced the Spanish tile foyer. Stepping out of the night into the brightness had a transforming effect on her mood.

Or perhaps it was her first sight of a radiant Abby Franklin. She was standing with a not-quite-so-comfortable-looking Steve Clairborne greeting guests. Her sweater-topped sequined gown seemed as natural on her as the tailored suits she often wore to work. While her fiancé was ruggedly handsome in a tuxedo, Jo suspected he'd like to rip off his bow tie and open the stud at his neck.

When he saw her, he grinned and shook his head. She smiled back and gave him a thumbs-up sign. Probably they were the only two people here who wished the Franklins had thrown a crab feast instead of a formal party. Except that it was the wrong month for crabs.

They embraced warmly. Jo had helped Abby save Steve's life six months ago when he'd come back to Baltimore from the Far East to investigate his sister's mysterious death.

He pretended to do a double-take as he inspected her expensive outfit, makeup and hairdo.

"Who is this mystery woman?" he teased.

"You didn't think I had it in me, did you?"

"Of course we did," Abby interjected.

"It's a lot different from your usual tomboy-next-door image. But I like it," Steve continued. "I think Cam will, too."

"Who's Cam?"

"Our best man. I'll introduce you later," Abby promised.

After a few more minutes Jo moved aside so others could talk to the happy couple. As she wandered from drawing room to conservatory to dining room, Jo looked for Laura Roswell. She, Abby, and Laura all had their offices downtown in a turn-of-the-century building at 43 Light Street. Abby was a psychologist, Laura a lawyer. The three women often helped each other out on tough cases. More than that, they were the kind of friends who could be counted on in a crisis.

Jo was on a first-name basis with very few of the glittering society crowd who filled the elegantly furnished rooms. But she'd seen a number of the faces on TV or in the newspapers. Most were in small groups talking and enjoying the hors d'oeuvres being passed on silver trays by elegantly dressed waiters.

She couldn't help feeling more of an observer than a participant as she snagged herself a tiny quiche. Finally she spotted Laura and was heading across the drawing room when she felt the fine hairs on the back of her neck prickle. Someone was watching her. She could feel it. Like the malevolent eyes of Eddie Cahill boring into her the last time she'd seen him.

It took all of her willpower to keep from whirling around and confronting the menace behind her. Instead she turned slowly and casually surveyed the room. A waiter gave her a half smile. No one else seemed to be paying her any special attention.

Stop it, she told herself sternly. *The Franklins didn't invite the bogeyman to the party.*

With a too-bright smile plastered on her face, she grabbed a glass of champagne and took several swallows before starting back toward Laura. But her path was now blocked by a knot of men recounting the details of a golf game.

She was debating another route when she felt something hard press into the small of her back.

"Don't make a move, sister," a sinister voice hissed. "I've got you covered."

Her body, already tensed for action, jerked. The champagne she was holding splashed onto the front of her green velvet suit.

"Oh, brassafrax," came a muttered exclamation. "Jo, I'm sure sorry." She recognized the voice, and relief flooded through her. Turning she found herself staring into the apologetic brown eyes of Lou Rossini, the former shipyard worker who was now the superintendent of

43 Light Street. His gnarled index finger was extended like the barrel of a revolver.

"Lou. What—?"

"Just a stupid joke. You ain't usually so jumpy."

When he tried to dab at the front of her suit with a cocktail napkin, she shook her head. "That'll just make it worse. I'd better go see what I can do."

A hair dryer would take care of the wet mess that spread across the front of her green jacket, Jo thought as she went to seek out her hostess. She met Abby first, who directed her up to the master bedroom and told her she'd find the appliance in the vanity in the dressing area.

After a quick thank-you, Jo scurried up the stairs. At the end of the hall, she stopped for a moment to gape at the elaborate bedroom that looked as if it had been transported from the royal palace in Madrid.

The hair dryer was in one of the deep drawers of the marble vanity.

Although Jo had never been particularly domestic, she had some dim idea that she should try to get the stain out with water. Wetting a hand towel, she dabbed at the front of the jacket and succeeded in making the nap of the velvet look like a cat after a swim.

Behind her in the bathroom, someone else was also running water. When the door opened, a tall, dark-haired man stepped into the dressing room.

In the mirror, her eyes collided with those of Clark Kent behind a pair of gray-rimmed glasses. He was the image of Christopher Reeve. Did Abby's family know him? They hadn't mentioned it, but it could be possible.

As she studied his reflection, she began to pick up differences. The features were a bit more angular. The hair was a little curlier. The eyes were gray instead of blue. Yet the face had that same irresistible quality that had made her heart flutter when Superman had taken Lois Lane for that first magical flight over Metropolis. She wondered if this guy would look as good in tights and a cape.

He seemed just as intrigued with her face as she was with his. Then his gaze dropped to the inland sea that spread across the front of her jacket and the washcloth in her hand. "You're going to ruin that."

"No kidding."

Reaching briskly inside his tuxedo jacket, he pulled out something that looked like a slightly flattened flashlight. Instead of a light bulb behind glass at the end, there was a cone-shaped opening.

"What's that?" Jo asked.

"The prototype for an ionization spot remover. It lifts out foreign matter by changing the charge in the fabric from negative to positive. Want to give it a try?"

"Do I get a money back guarantee?"

"Sure." He threw a switch and the device began to purr.

She'd expected him to hand it to her. Instead he crossed the three feet that separated them and began to run the cone-shaped end of the gadget back and forth across the front of Jo's jacket.

"Turn a little to the side." His other hand went to her shoulder. Both hands were long and tapered and almost graceful for a man. As he moved the device back and forth a quarter inch above the suit front, he pushed a rapid combination of buttons on a key pad along the top of the instrument.

"What are you doing?"

"Augmenting the rapid recovery factor. But I'd better separate the alpha and the delta functions."

"Right. Sure."

Jo rarely sat by and let other people take charge of situations. Now a combination of curiosity about the device and curiosity about the man kept her immobile.

Clark Kent's gaze was intense as he bent to the work. In fact, his absorption was total, as if his mind was capable of filtering out any extraneous elements—like the fact that his face was now in close proximity to her chest.

Searching for something to occupy her own attention, she noted that his nose was perfectly proportioned with the rest of his features. His lips were narrow and pressed together as he concentrated on the task at hand. Through the glasses, she saw that his lashes were long and dark, quite striking really.

Wondering why she'd gotten caught up in such details, she shifted her regard to the suit jacket. To her astonishment, she saw that the wet spot had almost vanished and the velvet fabric had recaptured much of its former luster.

"Hey, that thing really does work. Where'd you get it?"

"I invented it."

The strong fingers on her shoulder shifted her to a different angle, bringing her body more tightly against his. She was starting to feel hot. In the next moment she realized why. The fabric over her chest was steaming.

"Ouch."

"Sorry. Let me get it away from your skin." His attention was still on the stain removal operation. Without hesitation, his free hand slipped inside her jacket.

Jo was rendered temporarily immobile as his warm flesh came in contact with the silky fabric of her blouse. As his fingers shifted to press against her breast, she sucked in a quivery breath.

The other hand, which was still moving back and forth with the stain removal instrument, paused in mid-stroke. He raised his head, and his gray eyes locked with her green ones. For several heartbeats, neither one of them moved.

Clearing his throat, he withdrew the offending hand. "Sorry."

Was he?

"Listen, uh—thanks. It's almost as good as new, really," she was surprised to hear herself stammering. Snatching her evening purse from the vanity, she turned and made a swift exit from the dressing room.

Jo was halfway to the stairs when she remembered she hadn't planned to go directly back to the party. Now that her jacket was back to normal, there was a call she should make. Hopefully it would set her mind at ease. If it didn't, she'd know what she was up against.

She found a phone in the upstairs den. The number she wanted was in the address book she always carried, even in an evening bag. One of the things Jo had learned from her deceased husband, Skip O'Malley, was that the right contacts can make the difference between cracking a case and going down in flames.

Now she thumbed through the well-used book and found Sid Flowers's number. A senior administrator in the Maryland prison system, he was bound to know what was going on.

"Flowers here," he answered crisply.

"This is Jo O'Malley."

"Jo, where in the hell are you? I've left messages on your answering machines at work and at home."

"I'm at a party."

"I assume you know about Cahill."

"Can you give me the scoop, Sid?"

"The details are confidential."

"Understood."

"As near as we can figure it, he persuaded a fellow inmate to fake an epileptic seizure in the kitchen. Then, while everybody was watching the Academy Award winning performance, he slipped into the garbage room and killed the guard. Unfortunately, the truck went right to the Howard County dump. If we'd intercepted it fifteen minutes earlier, we would have had him in custody again."

"Then he's still on the loose, I take it." Jo was amazed at how steady her voice sounded when she could feel her nerves jumping like bullfrogs on a hot plate.

"It's only a matter of time before we pick him up."

"Meanwhile, I'd better watch my back." There was an electronic click and the line was suddenly stronger.

"Did someone hang up your extension?" Jo asked the correction officer.

"I'm here alone."

"Well, maybe somebody here picked up the phone and got hooked on the Cahill drama."

Flowers laughed. "If they're still on the line, they're under arrest."

Jo laughed too, but she felt the hairs on the back of her neck flutter again. Had someone been deliberately listening? No. Why would they?

"If anything else breaks, I'll let you know."

"Thanks."

"Jo..." Sid's voice was edged with concern. "Maybe you ought to consider taking a vacation until they catch up with Eddie."

"Don't be silly. I've got a business to run."

"Guess you do. This will probably blow over in a few days anyway. Either Cahill's in Wilmington by now, or they're gonna scoop him up PDQ."

"Have you talked to Karen Cahill or Jennifer Stark?"

"I'm working on it."

There were more reassurances proffered and accepted. But when Jo got off the phone, she closed her eyes and took several deep breaths. No matter what Flowers said or how tough she tried to sound, she wasn't going to stop looking over her shoulder as long as a psychopath like Eddie Cahill was on the loose.

Right now, however, her immediate problem was getting through the evening without any more mishaps. Piece of cake, she assured herself. How bad could an engagement party be compared to a killer on the loose?

Chapter Two

The ground floor was even more crowded when Jo came back down. For a moment she stood near the foot of the spiral staircase surveying the guests. Which one had been listening to her conversation with Sid Flowers, she wondered. Had it just been an innocent mistake? Or was someone interested in her personal business?

Laura Roswell's voice broke into her thoughts. "Jo. I've been looking all over for you."

"Likewise." They smiled at each other, two women from very different backgrounds who were closer than family now.

The blond lawyer was wearing an ice-blue beaded gown that could have been part of the Nancy Reagan designer loan program. With Laura's long legs and gentle curves, it looked much better on her than it would have on the former first lady. But it wasn't a loaner. Jo was pretty sure that Dr. William Avery, Laura Roswell's husband, invested in his wife's clothing as a reflection of his success.

"Where's Bill?" Jo asked.

Laura's expression tightened. "He's known about this party for weeks, but he decided at the last minute that he just had to attend an Internal Medicine meeting in Atlanta.''

Jo heard the mixture of annoyance and hurt in Laura's voice. Were her friend's marital problems building to some sort of crisis? She'd mentioned several times that things weren't going well with her and Bill.

''I'm sorry,'' Jo responded.

''One way or another, things are going to shake out,'' Laura predicted. ''But I'm not letting it get me down right now. This is Abby and Steve's night.''

Before they could continue the conversation, Abby's mother joined the pair. A tan, slender woman in her late fifties, Janet Franklin looked fit and attractive. If her mother were any indication, Abby was going to age gracefully, Jo thought.

''So there you are,'' Mrs. Franklin said. ''We're taking a few pictures in the library. And we'd like to photograph Jo with Steve's best man, Cameron Randolph.''

With that name he was undoubtedly another Baltimore blue blood, Jo thought. Was he a maverick like Steve, or had he carved himself out a comfortable niche with his silver spoon?

The matron turned to Laura. ''We'd like shots of everybody who's going to be in the wedding party.''

When they entered the room, the photographer was just finishing a series of romantic poses with Steve and Abby. The bride-to-be looked relaxed. Her intended looked as if he'd rather be back running guns into Afghanistan. When he saw Jo, relief washed over his face. ''Your turn,'' he called out, stepping out of the lights and tugging Abby along with him. The photographer was about to object, but she shook her head.

''I think he's reached his limit.''

Steve gave Abby a grateful hug.

"Okay, we can move on to the matron of honor and best man."

Jo quickly glanced down at the front of her jacket. It would pass inspection. As she positioned herself in front of the fireplace wall, a tall, rangy man who had been standing in the shadows stepped into the light. When his gaze encountered hers, she knew he'd been aware of her from the moment she'd stepped into the room.

Her stomach did a triple somersault.

"Jo O'Malley, I'd like you to meet Cam Randolph," Abby made the introductions, not realizing she was already twenty minutes too late. "I'm sure the two of you are going to get along famously."

"We've already met," Cam told Abby. "She was a reluctant guinea pig for one of my new inventions." When he spread his expressive hands, palms up, Jo remembered the feel of his warm flesh against hers.

"As a matter of fact he took the stain off the front of my suit," she added hastily. "Otherwise I'd be running away from the camera."

"Sounds intriguing," Steve interjected. "Are you going to tell us about it?"

"No," came the simultaneous response.

Abby looked from Jo to Cam. Before she could comment further, the photographer interrupted.

"Stand right here." He maneuvered Jo and Cam together. She slid him a sideways glance. His tall frame was stiff, his hands awkwardly clasped in front of him. So he wasn't quite as cool as he was pretending to be, she thought, secretly pleased.

The photographer stepped behind the camera and snapped off two shots. "Come on, you guys. Make it look like you're having fun."

Jo turned to Cam and gave him an exaggerated grin. "Play like you just won the Nobel Prize for stain removal."

He grinned back. "Right."

The photographer was able to snap off several pictures of a smiling couple. "Much better. Thanks, guys."

"Don't go away," Abby said as they stepped out of the lights. "We need you for the group shot."

They moved to a quieter corner of the room while the photographer selected his next victims.

"So how do you know Steve?" Jo asked, making an attempt to normalize diplomatic relations.

"We were at McDonough together."

Well, I was right, Jo thought. One of the city's most prestigious prep schools. Cam Randolph was definitely out of her league.

He must have read her doubtful expression. "I promise I won't spring any more inventions on you tonight."

"It's not you. It's the guy who escaped from prison this evening that I'm really uptight about." It was sort of a relief to joke about the danger.

"What are you talking about?"

"Eddie Cahill. A drug dealer I got mixed up with last year. Apparently the prison system couldn't hold on to him."

"How did a nice girl like you get mixed up with a drug dealer?" Cam sounded as if he suspected she might be pulling his leg.

"On a case. I testified against him."

"Are you with the police?"

"Private detective."

"Oh." His eyes narrowed and his expression closed.

Jo suddenly wished she'd kept her big mouth shut. It had a habit of getting her into trouble. "You have something against private detectives?"

"It's nothing personal." He cleared his throat. "If you're worried about escaped criminals, you should have a good home security system."

"I have one of the best. The Centurion from—"

"—Randolph Enterprises," he supplied.

Jo realized her mind hadn't made an important connection. "Your company?"

"Yes. And my design."

"Well, I love the auto-delay feature. And the tone sequence selector."

"It definitely gives you more for the money. But I try to build special features into all our products."

"Have you always been in the design department?" Despite herself, Jo was impressed. She'd seen the Randolph Enterprises catalog and knew the company offered a wide range of innovative merchandise.

"I had to take over management for a couple of years."

Jo caught a hint of tension in his voice but suspected he wasn't going to elaborate.

She was right. He changed the subject. "I'm back in the lab now."

"Do you have a lot of inventions?"

"Thirty-seven patents."

Jo whistled. "Maybe we weren't joking about the Nobel Prize."

"Not likely. Only a small percentage of inventions can be brought to market as profitable products. Since we don't have unlimited resources, sometimes I have to rely on Phil Mercer's judgment on where to put our priorities."

Again she caught an undertone of acerbity. "Who's Phil Mercer?"

"Our CEO. He was my father's right-hand man."

"Your father retired?"

"He died a few years ago."

The answer was clipped, and Jo understood why he might not want to pursue the topic. When you loved someone, it was hard to reconcile yourself to never seeing them again. Even after three years it still hurt to think about Skip.

They were called over for the group shot of all the participants in the wedding. Then dinner was announced. Jo pretended she'd agreed to eat with friends and joined a group of young professionals. As she picked at artichoke hearts vinaigrette she couldn't shake the tension headache Eddie Cahill had generated. Only a desire not to let Abby down kept her at the table, barely holding up her end of several sporadic conversations. Finally, just before dessert, she gave up the struggle and slipped away.

Outside Jo gave her keys to the parking attendant. Once he had a description of her car, he disappeared, and she was left standing alone under the arbor that spanned the circular drive. A tiny circle of light enclosed her. Beyond it the concealing darkness hovered. At least she didn't have to march out into the night again.

It had gotten colder during the evening, and the wind's icy fingers probed through her jacket. Once more she wrapped her arms around her shoulders to ward off the chill, yet she knew the wind and cold weren't the only reasons she was shivering. It was impossible to shake the awful sensation of being watched. She'd felt as if someone had been keeping tabs on her all night, playing hide-and-seek in the crowd.

Last time she'd played it cool. Now she whirled around, her eyes probing the windows on either side of the door. No one was peering back. But that hardly lessened the tension in her neck and shoulders.

She felt some of the strain melt away when she saw twin headlights cutting through the dark. As her car pulled in front of the door, she hurried around to the driver's side. Once behind the wheel, she gunned the engine and roared off down the drive.

She thought of Abby and Steve wrapped in the warmth and love of friends and family. But more importantly, they had each other. She remembered the feeling. Just for a minute she let herself wish there were someone around to take care of her—or someone at home who would breathe a sigh of relief when she walked in the front door. Then she shook her head. Except for the few years she'd been married to Skip, she'd always taken care of herself. There was absolutely no reason she couldn't continue.

Not until Jo was several blocks away did she stop to consider the uncharacteristic panic that had sent her hurtling down the Franklin drive like the Tokyo Bullet. She never acted like this. She was a woman who was perfectly capable of handling dangerous situations. That was what she did for a living. But something about the house or the party or the company had thrown her badly. Or perhaps it was just the threat of Eddie Cahill hovering over the proceedings.

As she drove back toward Roland Park, she went over each element of the evening but couldn't draw any firm conclusions. However, her mind kept coming back to Cam Randolph.

He was part of what had thrown her. In a man-woman way. But she wasn't looking for a relationship. And if she were, it wouldn't be with someone like him. They were worlds apart socially. Not to mention that he was one of the smartest guys she'd ever met. What in the heck were they going to talk about until the wedding was finally over?

She was still trying to puzzle that one out when she turned onto her street and reached for the automatic garage door opener. After the door had shut behind her, she got out of the car and punched in her I.D. code on the security system's key pad. The box played back a little tune that told her everything was as she'd left it. Suddenly she realized she wasn't going to be able to hear that melody without thinking about the inventor. She wasn't sure whether she liked that or not.

THE STASH HAD BEEN right where he'd left it, in the Eternal Friend Pet Cemetery on Route 1. Early Sunday morning had been a good time to disinter the grave marked Rambo. Back when Eddie had buried the little casket, he'd said he was putting a beloved poodle to rest. The watertight box had really contained twenty thousand dollars in small bills. Eddie had put the bread aside for an emergency when he'd been riding the crest of a wave of successful drug deals. He hadn't had any specific catastrophe in mind, but now he was damn glad he'd had the foresight.

Last night he'd stolen some coveralls off a Howard County clothesline and hitched a ride with a trucker to Jessup. At the cemetery he'd found a shovel in the groundskeeper's shed and dug up the dough. Then he'd checked into a rundown motel in Elkridge, where he'd scrubbed the garbage smell off his body. After that, he'd watched accounts of his escape on the evening news and gone to sleep with the guard's gun under his pillow.

The next morning he was feeling rested, refreshed and ready to settle a few scores. As he watched the news again, he chuckled. The money was going to make all the difference. Without it he'd just be a poor schmuck on the run. With it, he could buy what he needed and lay low until some of the heat was off.

Over an Egg McMuffin and a cup of black coffee, which he brought back to the motel room, he considered his options. First on the agenda were some decent clothes and some wheels. Then he'd think about the tools he needed. He already had a gun. Adding an assault rifle to his arsenal wouldn't be a bad idea.

JO O'MALLEY woke up determined to look on the bright side. As she retrieved the fat Sunday paper from the front walk, she counted her blessings. She owned her rambling old Roland Park house free and clear, thanks to Skip's mortgage insurance. She was self-supporting. And the police had probably already recaptured Eddie Cahill, although she wasn't going to spoil her Sunday morning by calling them until she'd eaten breakfast—just in case.

On weekdays Jo just grabbed a bowl of cereal and instant coffee in the morning. On Sunday she continued the ritual that she and Skip had started. Baking-powder biscuits, country ham, fresh ground coffee. They made her think of home and warmth and love. She did so in a positive way. There was no point in dwelling on what was missing from her life.

First Jo whipped up a batch of biscuits, then she opened the *Sun*. Since she'd been a kid in western Maryland, she'd always read the comics first. Usually her only concession to adult responsibility was to scan the headlines when she opened the paper, but this morning she read the article on Eddie Cahill. It had less information than she'd gotten from Sid the night before, so she turned to her favorite comic—The Far Side. Talking cows again. She grinned.

Her good mood lasted through two cups of coffee and a plate of biscuits smothered with butter and her mother's wild raspberry jam. Not a very low cholesterol breakfast, she thought as she went out to empty the trash. But one of the joys of living alone was eating what you wanted.

Halfway down the steps to the backyard, she stopped and uttered a rather unladylike imprecation. The trash cans lay on their sides, and the refuse looked as if it were scattered as far as the Baltimore County line.

Standing with her hands on her hips, she did a slow burn. Then she got a pair of garden gloves out of the toolshed and started picking up the debris from her well-tended yard. After Skip had died, she had assumed the upkeep of the three-quarter acre that surrounded the house would be a chore. Instead she discovered she liked pulling up weeds and planting flowers. She even had a garden down near the alley where she grew tomatoes and zucchini.

Muttering under her breath, she pulled a soup bone out from under the forsythia and a wad of clothes dryer lint off her favorite tea rosebush.

Mac Lyman, the retired postman who lived next door, came out to commiserate. Jo liked Mac. He reminded her of the honest, hardworking folks she'd grown up with in Garrett County.

"I guess those good-for-nothin' dogs got you again," he said as he began picking up scattered papers.

Jo stuffed a juice carton back in the can. "'Fraid so. Did they mess up your yard, too?"

"Not this time."

"You're lucky." Trying not to get her bathrobe dirty, she edged under a hydrangea to retrieve a plastic meat tray.

"Funny thing," Mac mused. "Usually I hear barkin' or somethin'. Not this time."

"You didn't see anything?"

"Zippo. No details." He waited for a moment. "Don't you get it? Details. Tails."

She forced a laugh. "Yeah. Right." She hadn't heard any barking, either. And she hadn't slept particularly soundly. Maybe it hadn't been dogs. But what else could have made such a godawful mess?

Jo tightened the belt of her bathrobe. All at once it was easy to picture a short, wiry man with Eddie Cahill's ferretlike face prowling around her house.

Come on, O'Malley, she chided herself. *What's happened to your deductive reasoning? If Eddie Cahill came after you, he wouldn't get much of a kick from scattering a little bit of garbage. He'd be scattering buckshot at the very least.*

With Mac's help, the trash was cleaned up in less than fifteen minutes. Jo thanked the old man warmly and went back inside to shower. Hot water washed away the outside chill, but it couldn't quite reach the cold feeling that had sunk into her bones.

WHEN CAM was deep into a new project, he couldn't stay away from the lab, even on Sunday morning. So after his regular five-mile run, he showered and pulled on a pair of jeans and a sweatshirt.

The outfit was modest. His Cross Keys Village town house was small but comfortable. The sleek red Lotus in the garage was one of the few luxury items he'd acquired. Although the Randolph fortune would have bought a life-style full of upscale perks, in general, material items didn't mean much to Cam.

He cared more about intellectual challenge and about having built Randolph Enterprises back up the Forbes' hot list.

Electronics was one of his true passions. So was maneuvering the Lotus down narrow Baltimore streets with the skill of a race car driver.

He hummed along with the radio as he made the twenty-five-minute ride from Cross Keys to Owings Mills. Pulling into the executive parking lot, he noticed Phil Mercer's Mercedes nearby. So the CEO was catching up on business again on Sunday, too.

Cam sighed. With any luck he wouldn't run into him. Phil was a good manager, excellent at handling day-to-day operations. It was just that the man had strong opinions about which projects to push. Often his decisions were driven by monetary considerations rather than the love and challenge of innovation.

In the workroom behind his private office, Cam brought up the computer specs for the little electronic spot remover. The thermostat was definitely out of whack, he thought as he typed in instructions for a two-minute simulation of the cleaning cycle.

While the results plotted themselves out on the screen, he realized he wasn't thinking about the temperature curve. He was recalling the soft curve of Jo O'Malley's breast under his hand.

Randolph, you've been buried in the lab too long, he told himself sternly, *if all it takes is a little inadvertent canoodling to make you react like a teenager at his first strip show.*

But even as he mentally tossed off the self-deprecating thought, he acknowledged that the response had been more than a case of overloaded circuits. There had been something very appealing about Jo O'Malley. The bouncy red curls, the impish blue eyes, and the slightly sassy manner. Most of the women he met were impressed with his money. He'd known instinctively that Ms. O'Malley didn't give a damn. In fact, the Randolph millions probably meant as much to her as mildew in the corner of the shower. He hadn't met many women like her, and he hadn't been sure how to parry her thrusts. Yet he'd enjoyed her unpredictability and the natural sex appeal she projected.

Being with her generated the same excitement as the start of a new lab project. You had a definite result in mind, but you didn't know how or if things were going to work out.

Just what kind of result did he want with Ms. O'Malley, he asked himself. As several very graphic pictures leaped into his mind, he fought to rein in his runaway imagination.

Slow down, he ordered himself. *There isn't any hurry.*

He and Ms. O'Malley were going to be spending a good deal of time in each other's company over the next few weeks. There wasn't going to be any problem getting to know her.

He forced himself back to work, but after another forty-five minutes he realized it wasn't going to be a very productive Sunday morning.

Getting up from the computer, he pushed a button that dispensed the right amount of instant coffee, water, creamer and sugar into a mug. After a robotic arm stirred it all together, the finished product slid toward him.

He took a sip. Perfect. His department had done a great job of programming the machine, but marketing had never gotten it into mass production. It was one of those products that had fallen through the cracks a few years ago when Randolph Enterprises had been on the brink of disaster.

That was a time he'd promised himself he wasn't going to think about. Now his Adam's apple bobbed painfully as memories came flooding back. It had all started when Dad had hired a private detective to find out who was responsible for the industrial espionage robbing Randolph of its most promising designs. The espionage had stopped, although there had never been any definite proof of who was responsible. But the price had been too high. Cam still blamed the detective who had exceeded his instructions when he'd dug into the mess.

Cam found his hand was clenched around the coffee mug. With a sigh, he relaxed his fingers, set the mug down, and walked to the window where he stood staring out at the parking lot.

His mother had died when he was only seven, and for years the three males in the Randolph family had been a close-knit unit. At least until Collin had— He clenched his teeth together and willed away the painful memories of surprise and shock. He loved his brother and would have stood by him. But Collin hadn't given him the chance. Shock had followed shock. Within the month, Cam had lost what remained of his immediate family— both his father and his brother. Ultimately, the only way to deal with the grief had been to shove the whole pitiful mess into a locked compartment of his mind. But there were times when the locked door came bursting open, and he'd be so enraged that only climbing into the Lotus and taking the precision machine up to 120 miles an hour could wipe out the need for retribution.

Why was all this coming back now when he was usually so efficient at keeping his dark emotions under control? He sighed. One thing he did know, mental connections didn't pop up at random. They were triggered by data stored in the brain—even if you didn't understand the correlations. However, there might be a way to get at the information.

Sitting down at the keyboard, he accessed the industrial espionage file his father had carefully kept. All at once, the grim facts flashed to life on the high-resolution screen. Documentation on the stolen development plans. Financial loss estimates. Status reports on the investigation. A couple of letters of reference on the detective Dad had hired. His name was Skip O'Malley.

Cam's eyes narrowed. Skip O'Malley. His conscious memory had deliberately lost the name. But it had been buried in his subconscious like a corroding container of nuclear waste.

He'd even talked to the man a couple of times, he remembered now. He'd been tough, experienced and in his forties. Now additional details were coming back to him. Several months after being dismissed from the Randolph case, Skip O'Malley had been killed in a waterfront shoot-out. Was Jo a relative? Perhaps she was the daughter who had taken over his business.

Although he didn't have a copy of the obituary, it was easy enough to retrieve it from one of the on-line data bases Randolph subscribed to. Five minutes later he was scrolling through the relevant section of the *Baltimore Sun*.

Cam's fingers froze on the keyboard. It was worse than he'd suspected. The little redhead who'd been occupying his thoughts that morning wasn't Skip O'Malley's daughter. She'd been his partner. And his wife.

He pushed back his ergonomically designed chair and meshed his fingers behind his neck. Well, this certainly put a different perspective on things, he mused, picking up a pencil and tapping it against his lips. Fate had handed him an opportunity, and he was never one to turn down that kind of gift.

The pencil began to seesaw between his fingers as his formidable intellectual powers kicked into overdrive. There were exponential possibilities, but he'd better consider his strategy carefully.

He was just starting to explore a promising plan of action when there was a perfunctory knock. Almost immediately, the doors to the lab swung open. Cam's head jerked around, and he found himself staring at Phil Mercer. The trim, gray-haired executive had a thick sheaf of papers under his arm.

As he advanced toward Cam, the scientist quickly blanked out the data on the screen. Theoretically he and management should be entirely open with each other, but he knew damn well that Mercer had his quota of hidden agendas. So did he, for that matter. The digging he'd been doing this morning was private—not something he wanted to share with the CEO.

"Glad I caught you today," Mercer was saying. "I've got some questions about your expenditures for the next fiscal year."

"I don't think they're out of line."

"I have the feeling you're not taking the present economic slowdown into consideration."

Cam sighed. Now he was in for a two-hour lecture on the delicate balance of profits versus R&D. Just when he was itching to start digging into the background of one Ms. Josephine O'Malley.

Chapter Three

Jo stopped by Laura Roswell's office Monday morning before unlocking her own door.

"How are you doing?" Jo asked Laura's secretary as she pulled off her ivory knit hat and gave her red curls a little shake.

"Fine." Noel Emery cut off the personal conversation to answer a phone call, which was interrupted by the second line. As she smoothly handled both conversations, she held up two fingers indicating that she wouldn't be long.

Noel ran Laura's office with top-notch efficiency. But it hadn't always been that way. When she'd first come to 43 Light Street, her self-esteem had been at rock bottom.

Jo had wondered why Laura had hired a secretary who lost messages and misfiled important briefs. All Laura had said was that the young woman needed the job.

It had been months before Noel told Jo what had happened at her last place of employment. Her boss, a partner in one of the city's most prestigious law firms, had pressured her into dating him. Next he'd tried to get her into bed. When she'd refused, he asked her to work late one night and raped her on his office sofa.

Noel had threatened to call the police, but he'd laughed and asked who she thought they were going to believe. She'd quit her job without a reference, and Laura Roswell had hired her when she'd been at the end of her rope.

With the encouragement of the other women at 43 Light Street, Noel had pulled her life back together. She was going to night school, and by day she guarded Laura's waiting room with the loyalty and tenacity of a bulldog.

Jo listened to Noel reading the riot act to a father who'd called to say he had no intention of coughing up child support payments. As she hung up, she rolled her eyes. "Laura's not in this morning. She's in judge's chambers on a custody case."

"Too bad. I wanted some free legal advice on canine vandalism."

Noel consulted her boss's schedule. "It looks like she has an opening around two. I'll give you a call if she can see you."

"Thanks."

Jo took the elevator up to her office. For a moment she stood in front of the frosted glass door panel that still proclaimed the occupants "O'Malley and O'Malley." It wasn't just sentiment that kept her deceased husband's name on the door and in the Yellow Pages. There were clients who still wouldn't hire a female detective. If they didn't ask about the other member of the O'Malley team, she'd let them assume he was an active partner in the business.

She smiled as she remembered back to when she came to Baltimore years ago. Like Noel, she'd been looking for a better job than she could find in rural western Maryland. Skip O'Malley, who'd been in desperate need of a secretary, had quickly discovered Jo didn't have much talent for office management. He'd fired her three or four times but always hired her back—because her insights often helped solve cases.

She'd become his de facto partner in six months and a real one in a year. A year after that, he'd given up fighting his attraction for a woman fifteen years his junior and married her.

Skip had taught her everything he'd learned in his twenty years of private investigation. More than a mentor, he'd been her best friend and lover as well. It would take a hell of a man to replace him. Certainly not Cameron Randolph, she told herself, and then wondered why she'd even entertained the idea.

Turning her attention to the blinking red light on the answering machine, she cleared a place on her desk, grabbed a yellow legal pad and a pencil and hit the button.

The first call was from Sid Flowers—but it predated their conversation of the night before. The second was from a prospective client who wanted to know if Jo worked on a contingency basis. "Sure," she muttered. "Plus up front expenses." She didn't take down the number. If the man wanted to call back, she'd explain her fee schedule.

The machine clicked again, and she raised her pencil to take notes.

"Hi there, Jo. Sorry I didn't catch you in." The words were friendly enough, but the voice was electronically distorted as if it might have been generated by a computer. Had those blasted direct marketing companies finally figured out a way to personalize their greeting, she wondered.

"You've got a gorgeous little body, angel face, you know that?"

Jo's head snapped around toward the machine. What kind of product were they selling, anyway?

"Just thinking about what I'd like to do to you makes me hot all over, baby. The problem is, I can't decide whether I want to give you a poke with my sugar stick or stick you with a hot poker." The observation was followed by a high-pitched laugh made shrill by the electronic distortion. The noise was like the buzz of malevolent insects. Jo felt them surrounding her, descending, crawling on her skin. Dropping her pad and pencil, she rubbed her arms as if that would rub away the invasion.

"Get the wordplay? But when you and me play, baby, it ain't just gonna be with words."

Jo continued to stare at the machine. Then she shook herself free of its spell. "Just who do you think you are, buster?" Still, her hand reached out and pushed the save button, a silent acknowledgment that the message had disturbed her more than she wanted to admit.

It was this damn Eddie Cahill business, she told herself vehemently. When she let her guard down, he had her feeling as if she were balanced on the edge of a razor knife.

Had he made the call?

She forced herself to think analytically. Whoever it was had used her first name, which wasn't in the agency's telephone listing or on the directory board in the lobby. It had to be someone who knew her—either personally or professionally.

That didn't mean it was necessarily Eddie. Over the years her job had put her in conflict with a fair number of people. But who would pick this method of getting even? If this was Eddie's little joke, maybe she'd lucked out. But she couldn't quite convince herself he'd be satisfied with long-distance vengeance. Not after the look he'd given her in court.

Was there some sort of clue to the caller's identity in the recording? Before she could change her mind, she replayed it, struggling to blot out the crawling feeling from the electronic distortion and listen dispassionately as she cataloged details. The caller sounded vaguely masculine, yet she knew that someone speaking into the right electronic equipment could make his voice sound like anything from Donald Duck to Darth Vader.

She ran through the tape one more time, listening for background noise. If the call had been made from a phone booth, there might be traffic sounds. She couldn't detect any. On the other hand, she thought she heard music in the background. Radio? Television? There was no way to tell. What would that prove, anyway?

Well, the last thing she was going to do, she told herself, was blow the whole thing out of proportion. There was no point in jumping out of her skin over a crank call. What she would do was get busy.

First she put in another call to Sid Flowers. He didn't have anything more to report—except that Jennifer Stark, the Assistant D.A. who'd prosecuted Cahill, was vacationing with her husband in the Virgin Islands.

"Lucky her," Jo muttered.

Flowers agreed.

Since the police weren't making much progress on the case, Jo decided to see if she could lend a hand.

Cahill. *C.* She opened the top file drawer and began shuffling through folders. Once she'd had the bright idea of color coding cases to make everything easy to find. Red for active, blue for deep freeze, green for paid up. Except that she'd gotten tired of transferring materials. So most of the folders were still red.

Cahill should be between Cable and Callahan. But the file was missing. Had someone been riffling through her papers? Before she could investigate, the phone rang.

It was Sandy Peters at the *Baltimore Sun*.

"Jo, the Carpenter family you were telling me about. My editor's interested. If you can get me those pictures and documents this morning, I think I can swing a feature for you on Sunday."

"You've got it. I'll meet you in fifteen or twenty minutes."

The Carpenters had been a family of five siblings. When the parents had died thirty years ago, the kids had been separated. One of the younger brothers had hired her to try to locate the rest of the family. Jo had posed as a social worker to get access to adoption records and had found two sisters and another brother. Then she'd started calling Maryland newspapers to see if they'd run a picture taken of the children when they were little—along with a human interest story on the search.

When she reached the lobby, Lou was cleaning the glass on the directory. Purple-blue light from the transom above the door pooled around him like a soft spotlight. "Some party last night, huh?" he observed.

"Right."

"You shoulda seen the baked Alaska flamin'."

"I had a little indigestion and went home early."

He gave her a closer inspection. "You do look kind of peaked."

"Thanks." Jo hesitated for a moment. "You haven't— uh—seen any strangers hanging around, have you?"

"Nobody any weirder than usual. Why?"

"There's this guy who escaped from prison last night."

"The one whose picture was in the paper?"

"Yes. I'm not on his Christmas card list."

"He's got a grudge against you or somethin'?"

Jo hated broadcasting her troubles. Yet in this case, she reasoned, the more people who knew about Cahill, the better. "I helped arrange for his state expense-paid vacation."

Lou whistled through uneven teeth. "Want me to keep an eye on the hallway outside your office?"

"If you happen to be up there."

Lou casually stopped his polishing and ambled to the door after Jo. She knew he was watching as she strode across the street to the garage where her blue Civic was parked. Beneath his crusty exterior, he was a real softy, she thought. He wasn't just someone who took care of an office building for a living. He cared about the tenants of 43 Light Street as if they were his children.

Lou watched Jo's back until she'd disappeared into the shadows of the parking garage. Perhaps if he'd waited until after her car pulled out, he would have noticed the gray van that drifted down the street in back of her.

The driver of the van wore workman's coveralls. A painter's cap partially hid his face. He looked like a handyman, but his talents were far more sophisticated. The interior of the van rivaled an FBI surveillance unit. There were directional mikes that could pick up a whispered conversation from across the street. And the computerized tracking system and racks of radio receivers, recording equipment and spectrum analyzers weren't found in any standard electronics catalogs.

He whistled an old Billy Joel song as he drove. His foot was light and easy on the accelerator as he kept the van several hundred feet behind Jo. He didn't have to keep her in sight. The directional finder he'd put on her car this morning was working perfectly.

He slowed down as Jo turned in at the fenced lot of the *Sun* complex and spoke to the guard at the gate. Instead of pulling in after her, he drove on by the redbrick building. No way was he going to explain his business to some rent-a-cop. But he did activate the directional mike and caught the second half of her conversation with the guard. She was dropping off material for a missing persons story. The coincidence made him laugh. The high-pitched sound echoed around him in the van, and he stopped abruptly. He hated it when his voice went all high and piercing like a dolphin in distress.

He checked his reflection in the rearview mirror. He looked like he was perfectly in control. And that's what he was. He swung around the corner and headed back toward the downtown area. He had time for a cup of coffee and a doughnut with cherry icing and sprinkles.

THE TWO-STORY LOBBY of the Sun Building with its black-and-white marble and stylized murals always impressed Jo, since the office of the weekly newspaper back in her hometown looked as if it hadn't been renovated since the Civil War. When you stepped through the glass-and-metal doors of the *Baltimore Sun*, you felt the power of the Fourth Estate. Which was just what she wanted, because the more people who saw the story on the Carpenters the greater the possibility of bringing the scattered siblings back together.

Sandy Peters thanked Jo warmly for bringing the file over so quickly. Getting out her notepad, she asked a few more questions about the case. "Can I quote you as the detective conducting the investigation? Or do you just want to be background?"

"Oh, what the heck. Go ahead and quote me. It can't hurt business."

There were so many aspects of detective work that churned up dirt and muck. It was nice to play fairy godmother for a change, Jo mused as she drove away from the newspaper building.

The sharp blast of half a dozen car horns made her body jump. With a sizzling bolt of awareness she realized she'd just turned the wrong way on a one-way street. Her car was facing four solid lanes of traffic—all coming toward her!

She did a quick U-turn on the wide avenue and sped back toward her office, pretending that the drivers in back of her weren't staring and that she didn't feel like an utter idiot. She'd sworn she wasn't shaking in her shoes over Eddie Cahill—and that she hadn't been rattled by the message on her answering machine. Obviously she was wrong.

Well, work was the best way to get back on track. Fifteen minutes later she was at her desk with the Cahill file, which she'd found stuck in the middle of another folder. She opened it just as the phone interrupted.

"O'Malley and O'Malley," she answered brusquely.

"Hello, Jo." The voice was thin and raspy and instantly flashed her back to the obscene call on the answering machine. In reaction, her scalp tingled.

"I called you, but—" the sandpaper voice continued. Jo cut him off before he could get any further.

"I will not tolerate being harassed," she spat into the phone. "If you try something like that again, buster, you're going to regret the day you ever messed with me." As she finished the warning, she slammed the receiver back into the cradle.

Fifteen seconds later, the phone rang again. Jo snatched it up ready to do battle again.

"Jo?" The same raspy voice inquired. This time she took a few seconds to make a rational judgment. It wasn't the electronic distortion she'd heard on the answering machine.

"Who is this?" she demanded.

The caller made an effort to clear his throat. "Cameron Randolph."

"Cam?" After she'd ducked out of the party, she hadn't expected him to call.

"I woke up with laryngitis."

"Oh, sheez. Cam, I'm sorry." A wave of relief mixed with chagrin washed over her. "I thought—"

"I take it you've been getting some—uh—offensive phone calls," he croaked.

"Just one. It's no big deal. How are you feeling?" She wasn't planning on talking about her problems to him.

"I'll live. This happens sometimes."

She pictured him in bed, alone, with no one to comfort him. "My mom used to give me honey and lemon when my throat was sore," she said softly.

"I've been using lozenges. Maybe I'll try your remedy."

"Do you need anything?"

He was silent for a moment. "I sound worse than I feel. Anyway, I should be all right by Thursday."

"Thursday?"

"You know, the party my aunt's giving for Steve and Abby. You didn't say whether you were coming."

Jo cringed. Maybe he thought she hadn't responded because of him. That wasn't the problem. She remembered getting the invitation weeks ago and sticking it somewhere safe. She'd simply forgotten to R.S.V.P.

For a moment she flirted with the idea of admitting her oversight and adding that she'd bought tickets to the

Baltimore Blast indoor soccer game, for that night. The excuse never made it to her lips.

"I was planning to come. Unless it's too late." Maybe circumstances would decide for her.

"No, no. We're all looking forward to seeing you. Especially me."

The last part wasn't very loud but it sent a shiver up her arms. Had he really said it? She certainly couldn't ask for him to repeat it. "I guess I should get directions," she muttered.

He cleared his throat again. "Why don't I pick you up?"

"I don't want to put you to any trouble."

"No trouble. Tell me where you live," he requested as if he hadn't already checked out the location of her Roland Park house.

Jo gave him directions.

"Then I'll see you around six-thirty on Thursday."

"Fine."

Jo hung up, surprised that she was actually looking forward to the party but still feeling a bit uncertain.

Cam hung up feeling slightly guilty, slightly nervous, and more than a little excited about the prospects for Thursday night.

JO DIDN'T HAVE TO WAIT until the afternoon to talk to Laura. She ran into her friend at the deli in the office building across the alley. Jeff and Mutt's specialized in upscale sandwiches like turkey with avocado slices and chopped liver with bacon. But when Jeff saw Jo come through the door, he slapped her usual hamburger onto the grill and lowered a basket of onion rings into hot oil.

Laura was just paying for a shrimp salad sandwich on five-grain bread. "Noel said you stopped by," she told

Jo. "I was going to call you as soon as I got back to my desk." She looked down at her sandwich. "But a conference in judge's chambers always makes me ravenous."

"How did you do?"

"We got custody. But we're still working out the child support. What did you want to discuss?"

"I need your advice about a neighborhood problem."

Laura looked out at the clear blue sky. "I was going to eat at my desk. But it's gotten so nice and warm this afternoon. There won't be many more days like this before winter sets in. Why don't we walk down to the harbor?"

"Sounds good."

As they strolled past the parking garage on their way to the refurbished inner harbor, neither woman was aware of the activity inside. The man who had been following Jo that morning was fine-tuning the modifications he'd made on her car. His tracking device was going to cause her some future problems. On the other hand, because he was otherwise engaged at the moment, he wasn't eavesdropping on the conversation between Jo and Laura.

Ten minutes later, the women arrived at the waterfront. Not so long ago the area had been littered with decaying factories and warehouses. Now luxury hotels, glass and steel pavilions, and plush office buildings proudly proclaimed the inner city's rebirth.

The pleasure craft that crowded the harbor in summer had departed, but the U.S. *Constellation*, the oldest ship in the U.S. Navy, still waited for the lines of children who came regularly on school field trips.

Half the downtown work force was taking advantage of the unseasonable weather. Jo and Laura were lucky to find a bench along the brick quay.

"What's on your mind?" Laura asked as she poked her straw through the top of her can of lemonade.

"Dogs. I'm thinking of strangling some," Jo quipped, aware that she was channeling her other anxieties into this particular problem.

"As your lawyer, I'd advise against it."

Jo laughed. "It was just a passing fantasy, but seriously, I do have a problem." Succinctly she explained about Sunday morning's backyard activities.

Laura commiserated. "But you can't accuse any dog owners unless you have proof."

"What do I have to do—stake out the area?" Before her friend could answer, her face lit up. "I've got it. I'll rig a camera with a motion detector."

Laura grinned. "I'm impressed. You really know how to do that kind of thing?"

"Piece of cake." She told Laura a bit about the technique.

"I could help you set it up this weekend."

Jo regarded her friend. They were closer than family but if Laura wasn't going to explain why she wasn't spending the weekend with her husband, she wasn't going to press, not when they only had a few minutes to talk.

"Great. At least that's one problem I can solve," she said instead.

"You have others?"

"Nothing I can't handle," Jo murmured.

"If you need help, you've got it."

"You, too."

Back at the office twenty minutes later, Jo finally reviewed the Cahill file. The notes brought back memories of the risky operation where she'd infiltrated the Baltimore drug culture to get the goods on him. If Eddie really was hanging around plotting to get someone, the person in the most danger was his ex-wife.

Karen was blond, beautiful, delicate, and not very independent. She'd been horrified at the chain of events that she'd set in motion by trying to prove that her husband was cheating on her. All she'd wanted to do was get out of the marriage with some of the money Eddie was throwing around like confetti at a New Year's Eve party. Instead she'd ended up testifying against him at a drug trial that had been page one news for weeks.

When Jo called Karen Cahill's home number, the phone just rang and rang. She was able to locate the woman on her next try—at her mother's Highlandtown row house.

"Jo, how did you figure out where I was?"

"I'm a detective, remember."

Karen clicked her teeth nervously. "If you can find me, Eddie can, too."

"You haven't heard from him? Or seen him?"

"No, thank God." Karen's voice quavered. "But he said he was going to get me. What am I going to do?"

Jo considered what advice to offer. Giving false assurances could be dangerous. On the other hand, she didn't want to make the woman panic. "It might not be a bad idea to get out of town until they recapture him."

"I just started dating this real classy guy. He's not going to like it if I disappear."

He won't like it if you get killed, either, Jo thought but didn't voice the sentiment.

"If you're going to stay in town, talk to the police about taking precautions."

"What precautions?"

"Don't go out alone. Check the locks on your doors and windows. Keep the curtains drawn at night. Let the police know if Eddie gets in touch with you." She went on to enumerate several other suggestions.

"I don't know whether I feel better or worse," Karen said. "I can't live my life like a prisoner. Tyler likes to go out at night. Dinner and dancing. You know."

Jo struggled with exasperation. This woman couldn't have it both ways. "Karen, just be careful," she advised.

"I wish I'd never met Eddie."

That was one point they agreed on, Jo observed silently. "Good luck," she offered instead.

"You, too."

After she hung up, Jo cupped her chin in her hands. Karen hadn't been much help. In fact, the woman had her priorities all screwed up. Talking to her had served an important purpose, however. It had made the danger more real.

Unlocking one of the bottom desk drawers, Jo brought out the snub-nosed .32 she rarely carried. After checking the action and loading the weapon, she put it into her purse.

Chapter Four

Jo kept several changes of clothes at the office for the various roles she needed to assume in her work. Over the years, she had played everything from a cocktail waitress to a nun to get information. Today after donning jeans, a plaid shirt and a bulky sweater, she inspected herself in the mirror. She'd do.

The solid weight of the gun felt reassuring as she left the office again. This time she was headed for Lucky's Cue Club, a pool hall just off Dundalk Avenue. Eddie Cahill had hung out there before he'd made it big, and from time to time he'd come back to hustle games and brag about his success.

Jo knew there had been a fair amount of jealousy among the old crowd in Eddie's former working-class neighborhood. In fact, a couple of his former buddies had testified against him. Probably they had a bet going on the time and hour he'd be picked up. If anyone at Lucky's had a lead on Eddie, perhaps they'd share the information. For a price.

In the garage across from 43 Light Street, Jo turned the key in the ignition and backed out of her parking space.

The moment her engine turned over, a warning signal sounded in a workshop ten miles away.

The man monitoring the alarm typed in a sequence of commands on his keyboard, activating a satellite link. Almost instantly, the high-resolution computer screen transformed itself into a grid map of the downtown area. The garage was at the center of the grid. As Jo's car began to move, the map changed so that a red blinking dot could follow her progress through the city. She was heading up Eastern Avenue. Where was she going?

LUCKY HADN'T SPENT much on exterior frills since the last time Jo had been to the pool hall hustling information about Eddie. The *L* on the neon sign in the window was still out. It had been joined in death by the *Y*. Now the sign simply said "uck." Which was a passable description for the dimly lit interior.

At two in the afternoon, the large room was just beginning to fill. A group of kids hooking school were in the back at the game machines, and the bar was lined with men in leather jackets and work boots. A lot of them were on unpaid vacation from the local auto plant.

The only other women in the place looked as if they weren't there to hustle pool. Ignoring the speculative stares, Jo bellied up to the bar and asked for a Miller Lite.

Before she'd taken more than a couple of sips, she was joined by a slim, dark-haired fellow who had been hidden in the shadows at the far end of the bar. He had the wolfish look of a ladies' man, but the broken veins in his face made him unappealing. Jo remembered him. In addition to women, he also liked his booze.

"What brings you to downtown Dundalk, beautiful?"

"You tell me."

His eyes flicked over her petite figure. "You're looking for a little action."

Jo stared back. "Guess again."

He changed tactics. "You're tryin' to get a line on Eddie Cahill." Apparently he also remembered her.

"Bingo."

"Eddie's too smart to show his puss around here."

"Is he still in town?"

The wolf man shrugged elaborately.

Jo pulled out the twenty-dollar bill she'd tucked into the side pocket of her purse.

Her companion studied the bill. Jo was pretty sure he wasn't trying to get a make on Andrew Jackson.

"You heard anything?" she asked.

Before he could answer, a younger guy who'd been listening to the conversation joined the group. His hair was shaved on the sides, stuck up on top, and hung in a long lock down the back of his neck making him look like an Indian chief. She liked his looks even less than the wolf man's. But she only wanted to talk to him; she didn't have to date him.

"Heard something about Eddie from a buddy of mine," he ventured.

"Yeah, what?" the wolf man demanded.

"This is between me and her." The newcomer glanced at Jo.

She nodded, and he lifted the twenty from between her fingers. The wolf man gave them a sour look before sauntering off.

When he had disappeared back into the shadows, the informant leaned toward Jo. "This friend of mine, Dick Petty, gets cars for people at the auction out at the fairgrounds. And other ways."

Jo didn't inquire about what the other ways might be.

"Eddie got in touch with him. Said he wanted a car. Nothing flashy or hot. But it has to be reliable. Said he'd pay cash."

"Did he give Petty a phone number?"

"No. He said he'd be back in touch."

"How can I get a hold of your buddy?"

"He's around, you know, but sometimes you can find him at Arnold's Gym up on Holabird."

"Appreciate it," Jo told him. If the information was true, it meant Eddie was still around town, and he had some cash. That was bad news.

At the door of the pool room, she turned and looked back at the man. He was drinking her beer.

Starting toward her car, she dug her keys out of her purse. At the corner of her vision, she saw a figure push away from one of the form-stone buildings and start toward her. She had a quick impression of spiked hair, black jeans and a black jacket with iridescent colors. Another punk.

She didn't want to stare; she didn't want to look intimidated. Yet something about the purposeful way he moved made her step briskly as she turned the corner and headed toward her car.

There was no one else on the side street, no one to help her, she realized as she bent to insert the key into the lock. A burst of movement and the instinctive knowledge that she had become a target made her turn and reach inside her purse. But she was a split second too late. Before her fingers could close around the butt of the gun, the leather strap over her arm fell away.

Cut, she thought, even before she saw the knife blade glint in the sun. Reflex took over.

The keys dropped from her hand. Fast as a whip, her foot lashed out with the technique she'd practiced in martial arts class. It caught her attacker in the thigh. He cursed. Then the knife was slashing down toward her arm. The blade sliced the knit of her sweater and pierced her forearm.

The slash sent a scream tearing from her throat. The stakes had escalated.

They were face-to-face: hers drained of blood, his covered with bumps and red splotches.

She was backed up against the car, and he had the knife. His fist grasped her purse. Why didn't he run? What else did he have in mind? Jo wasn't going to wait and find out.

"You slimebag," she shrieked as she launched her hundred-and-eight-pound frame toward him.

For a moment he seemed dumbfounded by the attack and her fighting skill. The two-second hesitation allowed her to kick the knife out of his hand. Now it was an even fight, she thought. Her brains and his strength.

She tried to wrestle her property out of his grasp, but she hadn't counted on his desperation. With one hand he clasped her purse against his neck.

Her fingers scrambled and clawed down his face. In the scuffle she vaguely heard her keys fall through the nearby storm drain.

With bone-jarring force, he slammed her back against the side of the car. As her knees buckled, he turned and ran.

Jo sat on the sidewalk, struggling to catch her breath. Now that the fight was over, she was aware of a burning pain in her arm. Looking down, she saw blood soaking into her sweater.

"Sheez!" No car keys. No purse. Cut and bleeding and sitting like a drunk on the sidewalk. She needed help, but she'd rather die than go back into Lucky's bar.

"You want an ambulance? Or the police?" someone asked.

She looked up to see an old man squinting at her from the front stoop of a house a few doors down.

"Could I use your phone to call a friend?"

"Yeah."

Jo grimaced as she pushed herself to her feet. In his living room, she called Abby and quickly explained her problem.

"Can you pick me up?" She gave the address. "Honk and I'll come outside."

"Sit tight," Abby said. "Help is on the way."

THE PURSE LAY on the passenger seat begging him to drag it over and riffle through the contents. He couldn't give in to the siren call until he'd pulled the van onto a side road where he knew he wouldn't be disturbed. Even if a car happened to pass, there was no reason to connect him to the mugging. When he'd used the transmitter to lead himself to his quarry, he'd parked well away from the pool hall. And Detective O'Malley had been in no shape to follow him back to the van.

Yet, as he made a sharp turn, he could feel his thigh throb. She'd studied self-defense. That's why she'd been able to get in a few licks. He'd be ready for that next time.

He was glad the windows were smoked glass as he unwrapped a cleansing pad and began to wipe off the makeup. She'd smeared the stuff, but he was sure she wouldn't recognize him in a police lineup. Only after his face was back to normal did he reach across the console and spill the contents of the purse out on the seat.

The pistol captured his attention. He thought she'd reached for a can of mace but she'd been going for a gun. The bitch could have shot him.

The brush with danger sent a little thrill down his spine like the caress of a lover's fingers. He sucked in a sharp breath.

Instead of just taking her purse, he could have bundled her into the van and taken her then. But that would have cut out half the fun. He wanted her to know he was after her. He wanted the terror to build until he was ready to strike.

The more you knew about a person, the easier it was to freak them out. And there were so many ways to collect information. With stiff fingers, he set the gun aside and began to poke through the rest of her stuff. Not much makeup. Just a lipstick. In one of those dumb colors women liked. Warm melon. He caressed the tube, raised it to his nose, smelled the faint cosmetic scent— and the scent of her body clinging to the cold metal. It made him feel close to her, very close. Just like her comb did. Pulling a bouncy red strand from the teeth, he wound it around his finger like a wedding band.

Her wallet was the biggest treasure trove. Baltimore Shopping Plate, phone credit card, VISA, gasoline cards, insurance, AAA, professional organizations. There was also a snapshot of a man. For several seconds he stared at the smiling image. Then he crumpled the photo in his fist.

He was going to make her sweat. She deserved it. Then, when he was ready, he'd strike with the coiled speed of a rattlesnake. Only there wouldn't be any rattle to give her warning. The thought made him giggle.

OUTSIDE A CAR HORN honked. Jo struggled to her feet, thanked her host once more and opened the front door. Shock had enfolded her injured body as she huddled in a faded wing chair. Now she grasped the railing to keep from toppling down the marble steps of the old row house.

A car door opened and someone rushed toward her. Not Abby Franklin. Cameron Randolph.

"What are you doing here?"

"Abby couldn't get away. She called me."

He was staring at her, taking in her white face, her tangled hair, the blood soaked through the arm of her sweater. His own face drained of color.

"My God, Jo. What happened?" As his hand gripped her good arm to steady her, his voice was edged with more than the hoarseness she'd heard earlier.

"A mugger. I'm okay. I just need—"

Her knees belied her words. They gave way unexpectedly, and she pitched against him. His body absorbed the shock as if it had been designed for that purpose. When he caught her and held her upright, one arm at her waist, the other across her back, she had the odd sensation of having come home.

Jo's head fell against his chest, and her eyes fought a losing battle to stay open. Walking down the steps had been a bad idea. She was on the verge of blacking out.

"I'm taking you to the hospital." Cam left no room for protest. For a moment, she gave in to his care, shocked at how good it felt. Even as he spoke, he was carrying her to the sports car and settling her in the seat.

She leaned into the comfort of the sun-warmed leather, only peripherally aware of him climbing into the driver's seat. In the next moment, the car accelerated like a jet going through the sound barrier.

"Are you sure I'll live to make it to the hospital, Mr. Sulu?" she managed in a weak voice.

"Is there ever a situation when you can't come up with a smart remark?"

"A few."

She cast him a sidelong glance as he wove expertly in and out of traffic. She would never have imposed on him like this. Yet when Abby had called him, he had come charging down here to help her as naturally as if they'd been friends for years. No, more than friends.

"I thought you were sick," she muttered, still not quite acclimated to his presence or the situation or her reaction to him.

"I'm better."

He had her to Francis Scott Key Medical Center in record time.

"Can you stand up by yourself?"

"Of course I can stand up!"

But her steps were still none too steady as he escorted her in from the parking lot. When she reached the desk, she realized she had a big problem. "Damn."

"What?"

"No medical insurance card, no ID and no money."

"I'll take care of everything."

"Cam—"

"We'll settle up later."

The admitting nurse had called the police, so while Jo waited for treatment, she made a brief report. She and the officer agreed that there wasn't much hope of getting her personal property back.

Finally her name was called, and she was ushered into a curtained-off cubicle. It was still half an hour before a nurse practitioner came in to stitch and bandage her wound.

She had told Cam she didn't need him anymore. He was sitting in a hard-back chair watching the doorway. As she came back into the waiting room, he jumped up.

"How's the arm?"

"I'll live."

Wordlessly, he took off his jacket and draped it around her shoulders. Now that the emergency was over, they faced each other uncertainly.

"Thanks," she murmured.

"I'd better get you home."

When they stepped out the door, she was astonished to find that it was dark. She'd been here for hours.

As the car headed northwest, she found she was almost back to normal—except for the throbbing of her arm and the oddly tight feeling in her chest as she sat next to Cam Randolph. It was because she didn't like being helpless or dependent, especially with him, she told herself. Well, it was only for another fifteen minutes. Ignoring the pain and the man beside her, she started cataloging the things she'd have to do: call her insurance company about the credit cards, get some money from the bank, talk to the DMV, report the theft of the gun...

The car had pulled in at a shopping center on Cold Spring Lane. "What are you doing?" she asked in surprise.

"Getting dinner."

"Cam, really, you don't have to do that."

"I want to. Do you like Chinese food?"

"Yes, but you don't—"

He got out of the car before she could argue any further. She sat with her arms folded, less and less pleased with the way he had taken charge. It was one thing to come to her rescue. It was another to— She stopped herself. The least she could do was accept his offer graciously.

When he returned fifteen minutes later and she caught the scent wafting from the bag he carried, she felt her stomach rumble.

Minutes later, they pulled up at her door, and she hurried up the front walk. However, when she reached the door, she stopped abruptly. No key.

"You're going to have to get the locks changed."

"Not unless that son of a gun digs them out of the storm drain. That's where they landed in the scuffle."

"At least you don't have to worry about his breaking in. But *we* might have to."

"There's a spare key at my neighbor's. I'll be right back."

After Jo opened the door, Cam didn't immediately follow her inside. She turned and found him studying the control panel for the security system. It wasn't the kind of thing she'd expect from most guests. But then the man had designed the thing, she told herself.

"It's a B9N8-150. We don't make that model anymore."

"Doesn't it work right?"

"Of course it works right! Correctly. It's just that we've incorporated some new features."

"Like throwing unwanted visitors off the porch?"

He laughed. "You need the inventor around to do that for you." He looked at her disheveled appearance. "Want to clean up before we eat?"

"Yeah."

"Are you up to sitting at the table? I could bring you up a tray."

"No! I'll come down," she answered quickly.

"I'll put the stuff in the microwave."

Upstairs she stripped off her clothes and washed away the street grime as best she could without getting the bandaged arm wet. Anything she put on was going to hurt. She settled for one of Skip's old sweatshirts over a pair of jeans. It was too much effort to pull on shoes and socks so she stuffed her feet into her bunny slippers.

Cam was in the living room when she came back downstairs, looking through Skip's collection of twentieth-century fiction. Her husband had been into Faulkner and Hemingway. She read the detective stories.

When he heard her footsteps, he turned. "Are you all right?"

"Do I look all right?" The minute she'd said the words, she was sorry.

She'd invited his inquisitive eyes to make an inspection. He started with the hair she'd quickly combed and progressed to the oversize sweatshirt and worn jeans. It ended abruptly at the bunny slippers. She'd thought the outfit wasn't in the least bit sexy; somehow his look of male appreciation made her feel otherwise.

In the car, she'd deliberately turned her mind to practical matters. Now that they were alone in her house, she was conscious that he was her first male visitor in a long time and that her hands were trembling slightly. She shoved them into her pockets.

He cleared his throat.

Her gaze swept up to meet his gray eyes. Men in glasses weren't dangerous, she'd always said. Who was she kidding? She knew he was just as aware of the sudden intimacy of the moment as she.

She took a step back, then quickly turned and headed toward the scent of Chinese food drifting in from the kitchen.

He watched the back of the baggy sweatshirt disappear into the kitchen. The way it swallowed up her slender form was endearing. The effect shouldn't be sexy but it made his body tighten. Maybe stopping to buy dinner was a mistake, after all.

The shirt was probably her husband's, he realized, and felt an unexpected stab of something he didn't want to label as jealousy.

Uncertainly he followed Jo down the hall. When Abby had called him, he'd decided she was handing him a golden opportunity to check up on Ms. O'Malley. That was before he'd seen her as pale as death and soaked with blood. Or before she'd pitched into his arms and he'd caught her slender form against the length of his body.

Jo moved a new Dean Koontz novel and a stack of bills off the kitchen table and onto the radiator and then got plates and cutlery.

The clutter made her self-conscious. At the moment everything made her self-conscious.

The house and furnishings had been Skip's. They were both comfortable in a warm, unconventional way. When she'd first seen the place, she'd assumed he'd acquired furniture on a need-to-use basis. There wasn't any particular style and nothing much matched. Most women would have launched a reform movement, but she hadn't cared enough about home decor to make any major changes. Besides, it was luxurious compared to the rural poverty in which she'd grown up.

Cam had turned to study the old-fashioned chestnut cabinets she and Skip had kept when they'd put in new appliances.

"The furnishings don't look very—" He searched for the right word. "Coordinated."

She laughed. "My husband's special brand of decorating."

"Oh."

They both busied themselves pulling out cartons and inserting spoons.

Eating, that should keep them out of trouble, Jo thought.

"I hope you like it hot and spicy." Damn, he hadn't meant it to sound that way.

"Um. But Skip had ulcers so we could never share any Szechuan dishes." As she finished the sentence, she realized she'd just mentioned her husband two times in as many minutes. It didn't take a Freudian analyst to figure out that subconsciously she was trying to warn Cam off.

She looked up to find the man in question studying her again. Their eyes searched each other. She was the first to lower her gaze.

"He was a lot older than you were."

Somewhere in her mind, the remark registered with more than face value. She was too off balance to grapple with the implications. "Fifteen years," she clarified.

"Did he teach you a lot?"

There was more than one interpretation to the question. "Like what?"

He watched her bite into a piece of chicken and then couldn't tear his eyes away as she flicked out her tongue to remove a bit of sauce from her lip.

He needed to know how deeply she'd been involved with Skip's cases. He couldn't stop himself from wondering about the sexual side of their relationship. How had the difference in their ages affected that? "Detective stuff," he clarified, his voice a shade raspier than before.

"He taught me everything I know."

"You worked closely with him?"

"Usually. Sometimes we had our own cases." She could remember a couple of times when he'd told her it was best for her not to get involved in what he was doing. She didn't see any need to go into explanations with Cam.

They were both silent as they concentrated on the food. Jo chewed and swallowed a mouthful of crunchy meat. "This is good."

"Crispy beef. In Chinese cuisine, the beef dishes are usually the least rewarding. But if they make this one right, it's wonderful."

"Do you know a lot about Chinese cooking?"

"I didn't mean to sound pedantic. It's just that when I get interested in a subject, I tend to go a little overboard."

"It's okay. Skip was like that, too, sometimes."

Cam wasn't sure he liked being compared to her late husband. "He made a study of Chinese gastronomy?" he asked stiffly.

"No. He knew everything there was to know about firearms and baseball."

The man on the other side of the table didn't reply.

"What do you—uh—do for fun?" she asked.

"The same thing I did when I was a kid. Tinker with stuff. Only now I'm designing new products instead of taking apart the family appliances or fixing things that don't work."

"That doesn't sound too relaxing."

"Well, in the evening I've got a stack of mysteries beside the bed."

Her eyes lit up. "Me, too. I like the women detectives best."

"I'm more into police procedurals. The logic appeals to me."

It would, Jo thought. She considered telling him that she was thinking of writing a book herself. But he'd probably just laugh.

As they finished the meal, they continued the literary discussion, both relieved that they'd found a safe topic.

Jo was reaching for a little more crispy beef when she saw the carton was almost empty. They'd put away an awful big meal.

"I never thought of Chinese food as a substitute for chicken soup." She grinned.

"Chicken soup?"

"Didn't your mother bring you bowls of chicken soup when you were sick?"

"I hardly remember my mother. Dad and Collin weren't much into cooking."

"Your mother—"

"Died when I was seven. Dad and my older brother, Collin, raised me." As he delivered that last piece of information, his face was watchful.

"I guess I'm not the only one who had it rough," Jo murmured. She didn't elaborate. Neither did he. Instead they both got up at the same time to start clearing the table. His hand brushed against her sleeve and she winced.

"Sorry."

"You should have told me it was still hurting."

"I'm okay."

"Did they give you anything to take?"

"I don't need anything."

He reached out and gently grasped her shoulders. She glanced down at his strong, lean fingers on her sweatshirt.

"If you need to take something so you can get to sleep, go ahead and do it. You don't have to tough out the pain."

She looked away, embarrassed that he'd read her so accurately.

"You're not used to having someone take care of you."

"I'm out of the habit."

"I never got into it."

She might have asked why. He hurried on. "You didn't like my showing up instead of Abby to take you to the hospital."

"She's already seen me at my worst. I guess you have, too—now."

"I like you at your worst as much as I liked you all spiffed up for Abby's party."

"Sure."

His hands dropped back to his sides. "Listen, I should probably let you rest."

"Well, thanks—for everything."

"See you Thursday."

"I'll be looking forward to it." As soon as she'd said the words, she knew they were true.

"I will, too."

They stood regarding each other for a moment. She saw his gaze drop to her lips. Seconds stretched or was it only her imagination that drew the moment taut. Then he turned abruptly.

She followed him down the hall and locked the door behind him.

The unexpected dinner with Cam had been edged with a man-woman awareness Jo didn't really want to examine too closely. They'd each been reluctant to reveal too much about themselves—except just before he'd left when she'd found herself admitting things she usually kept to herself. Jo was too worn out to ponder the implications.

Fifteen minutes later she had settled down in bed with the book she was reading. The phone rang, and she automatically picked up the receiver.

"Hello."

"Hi there, angel face. I'm glad I caught you. It's about time we got a little more up close and personal."

That voice! It was him again! Jo's spine tingled as if icy fingers were walking down her bones.

"Who—who is this?" she demanded.

The high-pitched laugh assaulted her again like swarming bees. This time, their stingers penetrated all the way to her marrow.

"Want to meet me at the Giant Food Store at the Rotunda Mall? We can see if the bananas are ripe."

"No!"

"You didn't tell me you liked M & M's. They're one of my favorites, too."

"Who are you?"

"Someone who's going to have his way with that gorgeous little body of yours," the caller continued. "It's going to be a lot of fun. We'll smear warm melon lipstick on your mouth, and you can leave love marks all over my skin. Unless you'd rather use those little white teeth of yours."

"No!"

Jo slammed down the phone. Her whole body had begun to shake. She felt physically assaulted. Invaded. Not just by the sexual threats, but by the mundane details of her life he'd tossed out at her. To keep her teeth from chattering, she clamped them together.

Ten seconds after she hung up, the phone jangled again. She let it ring. When the answering machine clicked, she shut that off too. Pressing her hands over her ears, she squeezed her eyes shut, drew up her knees under her nightgown, and huddled in a ball under the covers. Yet now she couldn't blot out the awful knowledge that the first call to the office hadn't been a fluke. This one was to her home number. Someone was stalking her. And he knew exactly where to find her at any minute of the day or night.

Chapter Five

Before going to bed Jo unplugged the telephone jack in her room. But she wasn't able to sleep. Questions with no answers circled in her head like caged animals desperate for freedom.

Who was calling her? What did he want?

She tried to stop thinking about the threatening words. They were burned into her brain tissue. The caller had mentioned the Giant. Had he seen her buy M & M's? And he knew the color of her lipstick. Was he someone who had been watching her? Or was he talking about the lipstick that had been in her purse? Did he have her Giant check-cashing card?

Panic jerked her to a sitting position. As chill air hit her shoulders, she clutched the covers up to her chin. The sudden movement jarred her injured arm, and it began to throb.

She'd been mugged this afternoon. When she'd clawed his face, his splotchy complexion had come off on her fingers. He'd been wearing makeup. Could it be the same man who was calling her? Was it Eddie Cahill? Was that why he'd been disguised?

She'd certainly baited him by invading his territory. If he had her purse, now he knew a whole lot more about her. Driver's license. Credit cards. Medical ID. Insurance. Oh God, he had everything. Except her keys.

Suddenly it was impossible to sit there in the dark, and she switched on the light beside her bed. For a few moments she squinted in pain. Then her gaze shot to the curtains that were pulled across the window. He could be out there now. Did it give him a charge to know she'd turned on the light? Was he laughing at her?

Stop it, she told herself firmly. *You're making more out of this whole thing than it's worth. The calls and the mugging probably aren't connected. Nobody's out there in the night under the hydrangea bushes watching your house.*

The ludicrous image called forth a brittle laugh. At least she could still joke about it, Jo told herself. That was a good sign. Getting out of bed, she crossed to the bathroom on legs that weren't quite steady, turned on the water, and filled the glass that sat beside her toothbrush holder. A few swallows of cold water made her feel better. Compromising, she left the bathroom light on when she returned to bed. She didn't fall asleep until just before dawn.

The face that greeted her in the bathroom mirror showed the effects of the sleepless night. Grimacing, she vowed she was going to take control of the situation.

Jo dug out her spare set of car keys and called a cab to take her to the Department of Motor Vehicles for a duplicate driver's license and registration. With that taken care of, she tackled her next problem—getting her car, although the thought of going back to Dundalk was as appealing as a trip to the dentist for a root canal.

Marching to the phone, she called another cab. After she'd slid into the back seat and given the driver the address, she leaned back and closed her eyes.

"You okay, lady?"

"Fine." Jo sat up straighter and pretended interest in the business establishments along the highway. She was actually picturing faces. Eddie Cahill the way he'd looked at her before they'd dragged him off to jail. The mugger with his punk haircut and makeup. She couldn't make the two images match up.

"What address did you say?"

"In the next block. You can pull up in back of my Honda." As the cab drew abreast of the spot where she'd been assaulted, she felt a hundred fists clench in her stomach. She knew the fear was ridiculous. The mugger wasn't hiding around the corner.

"Would you mind waiting until I check my car?"

"I can't stay long."

She slapped another five-dollar bill into his hand. "Indulge me."

First she peered into the storm drain. As far as she could tell, the keys were probably in the Chesapeake Bay by now. Then she turned to her car, inspected the tires for slash marks and started the engine. When she was satisfied, she gave the driver the high sign and roared out of the parking space at Cameron Randolph velocity. It felt good to put distance between herself and the scene of the crime.

But she still hadn't regained her equilibrium. The closer she got to her office, the more she found herself picturing the answering machine crouched on the bookcase like an animal poised to spring. Relief flooded through her when she saw that there weren't any messages waiting.

Flipping through her Rolodex, Jo found the number of the employee at the Chesapeake and Potomac Telephone Company business office who'd been helpful when she'd handled harassment cases for clients.

"Haven't heard from you in a while," Sheila Douglas replied to her greeting. "I guess you're still in the detective business."

"Yes. But this time I'm not making inquiries for a client. I've gotten a couple of nasty calls myself."

The woman made sympathetic noises.

"I know you ask customers with harassment complaints to keep a log for a week. But assuming the calls continue, I want to understand my options."

"Are there any distinctive specs?"

"Yes, the voice was electronically distorted. I got one message on the answering machine and one in person."

"An answering machine. That's not typical. Usually telephone harassers want a live reaction on the other end of the line. Let me try a couple of searches of our new computer base."

In a surprisingly short time, Mrs. Douglas was back on the line. "I did find some incidents that might be related. But it's not procedure to give out that kind of information without written authorization. I'll need to check with my supervisor."

"I'd appreciate that."

"Meanwhile, we do have some new tools to fight telephone misuse. Maryland is one of the states where you can get a caller ID phone that displays the number from which a call is placed."

Mrs. Douglas launched into an enthusiastic sales pitch for the new equipment. "Or, if you think the problem is serious enough to bring in the police," she went on, "you can take advantage of the new tracing option in the system. After the call is completed, you dial a special number that initiates the trace. The results are sent directly to the police department.''

''I guess I'd like to start with a caller ID phone.''

''We don't sell the equipment, but I'll give you the number of the company that does.''

After thanking Mrs. Douglas, Jo phoned the supplier and found she could get the attachment on her business and home lines by early the next week. She hung up feeling optimistic.

There were several more things she should take care of. Yesterday she'd been ready to go over to Arnold's Gym and look for Mr. Petty. Now she reconsidered the idea. After a silent debate with herself, she admitted that Jo O'Malley, P.I., wasn't too enthusiastic about putting herself in danger again. Instead she called Sid Flowers, who promised the police would follow up on the lead.

Over the next couple of days, Jo felt steadily better. She'd planned to talk to Abby about the psychological profile of telephone harassers. But there weren't any additional phone calls, so she didn't bother her friend with the problem. There also hadn't been any more news about Eddie Cahill. Perhaps he'd decided to cut his losses and get out of town after all. Maybe he'd even left the country. Or the planet!

Wednesday night Jo crawled into bed early, determined to catch up on some of the sleep she'd missed lately. Her light was off by ten forty-five, and she was asleep by eleven.

She dreamed of Cam. They were at a dance, swaying together to the music, their bodies drawing closer and closer. Her arms circled his neck. She tipped her mouth up to his. Their lips met, and she felt a warm surge of pleasure. Then he and the dance floor were gone, and she was alone in an endless park.

She was hurrying among beds of bright columbine, searching for him, when the flowers caught her attention. She had thought they were real; now she saw they were made of tiny wires, little filaments, electronic parts. Bees flitted between the blooms. Jo gasped as she took a closer look. The bees weren't what they had seemed, either. They were miniature robots with tiny glowing electric eyes like digital displays. Their silicon wings were veined with printed circuits.

But it was their mechanical hum that made her scalp crawl. *Bzzzzzzzzz.* It was the sound of danger. The laugh from the answering machine. Slowly, afraid to run, lest she attract their attention, she began to back away.

It was no good. Her skin prickled as more and more of the bees stopped moving among the grotesque flowers and hovered like toy helicopters—their green eyes all locked on her.

Fear choked her throat now. The fear swelled as the tiny robots rose from the flowers, circling and buzzing in a huge swarm. They poised in the air, the sun reflecting off a thousand beating wings. The whirring grew louder.

Desperately she turned to run. But too late, too late. Giant metal spikes sprang up to block her way. The bees were swooping toward her.

For what seemed like an eternity, she fled for her life, dodging the spikes. Her feet pounded the ground. Her breath hissed in and out of her lungs. But it was no use. She couldn't outrun them.

They overtook her, buzzing, whirring, diving for her arms and face, stinging her flesh, choking off her breath.

Scream after scream tore from her lips. Then she was sitting bolt upright in bed, heart hammering, sweat pouring off her body.

It took several moments to convince herself she was safe in her own room. But the noise hadn't stopped. Then she realized what she was hearing. It was the buzz and whir of the automatic garage door opener. Opening and closing, opening and closing by itself. The sound must have triggered the awful dream.

It was a relief to focus on reality. The damn door was on the blink. Or maybe it had been activated by an airplane radio frequency. Unless—

No. It must be a plane, she assured herself. The problem had occurred once before, and Skip had had to change the frequency on the opener. Tonight she'd have to turn it off.

The clammy fabric of her nightgown clung to her body as she eased out of bed. Stripping it off, she tossed it on the chair and found another in the drawer. Then she donned her robe and slippers.

In days past she wouldn't have hesitated to investigate a weird noise in the middle of the night. Now she couldn't afford to take any chances. Before going downstairs, she slipped Skip's .357 Magnum into the pocket of her robe. Then she turned on every light she encountered as she moved through the house.

Her ears were tuned to any unusual noises. She almost expected to catch the sound of insects buzzing. But all she heard were her own footsteps creaking on the old floorboards. Even the malfunctioning door had stopped whirring.

When she reached the entrance to the garage, she hesitated, picturing an intruder crouched in the shadows.

First she turned on the garage light. Then she shouted a warning through the door. "The police are on their way. And you'd better get the hell out of there." No response came from the garage. Still, she was holding the gun in a police assault stance as she threw the door open.

It took only a few seconds to determine that the garage was empty—except for her car. Even after she'd turned off the door and gotten into bed, she lay awake staring into the darkness conjuring up an electronically distorted laugh. Or was it the buzzing of a thousand bees?

JO HAD PLANNED to come home early Thursday afternoon to get ready for the party, but a new client walked into her office at four-thirty. The woman was in tears because her husband of three months had cleaned out their joint bank accounts and skipped town. Jo spent an hour and a half calming her down and getting as many facts as possible. However, there was nothing she could do about starting to trace the man until Monday.

By the time Jo got home, she was running late. She was about to dash upstairs when she remembered the mail. Along with the usual assortment of letters and bills was a package wrapped in brown paper. A note from her neighbor Mac Lyman was attached.

"A catalog company was offering a special on these things. They're guaranteed to keep unwanted animals out of your yard. If it works, we won't be picking up any more trash."

Jo smiled. That was certainly sweet of Mac to have ordered one for her. She'd have to insist that he let her pay him. She wanted to open the package and take a look at the device. But right now she'd better get ready. Or Cam was going to come over and find her still dressed for work.

After a quick shower, Jo used the blow dryer on her red curls and put on a little makeup. But she'd always been a sucker for gadgets, and the package downstairs kept tugging at her curiosity. Maybe she could spare a few minutes to open it. If it wasn't too hard to operate, she might even be able to get it set up outside before she left. But she'd better do it before she got into her dress.

After shrugging into Skip's robe, Jo padded downstairs in her bunny slippers. Bringing the package to the couch, she sat down and began to undo the wrapping. The unmarked cardboard carton inside was held together by two thick rubber bands.

Jo slipped the bands off, and the packing material fell away. She found herself sitting with a box about the size of a five-pound bag of sugar. Hefting it, she noted that the weight was about right, too.

Danger. Her intuition screamed a warning. She pictured herself hurling the box through the window. In her mind she saw it smashing against the sidewalk. But her body didn't carry out the command.

As far as her senses could detect, nothing happened. There was no noise from the box. No odor. No change in temperature. No flashing lights. No electrical discharge. No explosion.

But she felt as if an explosion had gone off inside her head. Somehow she *knew* that the box was the source of the sudden terrible pain.

Get away, her brain screamed. With a superhuman effort, Jo stood up. Her legs were no stronger than flower stems. Before she could take a step, her knees buckled, and she collapsed to the floor. As the box bounced beside her on the carpet, shock waves reverberated in her head. She tried to scream. No sound came out. The agony was locked inside her throat.

Get away. Arms and legs twitched. They wouldn't obey her commands. She lay on her side, helpless, disoriented, a prisoner in her own body—and more terrified than she'd ever been in her life.

TWENTY MINUTES later when Cameron Randolph rang the bell, there was no answer. He rang again and, to deny his own feeling of nervousness, waited with tuxedo-clad arms folded across his chest. When he still didn't get any response, he turned and looked back toward the street but didn't see Jo's car. It could be in the garage. Or maybe she had forgotten about the party. His stomach tightened with a mixture of disappointment and annoyance. He'd already told himself all the reasons why he shouldn't be attracted to Jo O'Malley. This was one time when his emotions didn't yield to logic.

He could see a light on in the living room. Cupping his hands against the glass, he peered inside. A figure lay crumpled on the rug in front of the couch. Through the window he saw a man's robe. Below it protruded the bunny slippers he remembered. Above it was flaming red hair. Jo. Her hand was stretched toward a black box that lay beside her. The box was sickeningly familiar.

"Jo," he called and banged on the glass. "Jo."

He couldn't see her face. She didn't stir, and he felt a knot of unexpected fear tie itself inside his chest as his eyes riveted on her limp body. My God, he hadn't anticipated anything like this! How long had she been lying there?

His first impulse was to smash through the window. He stopped himself. In his pocket was the new tool he'd been working on to test Randolph Electronics security systems. It wasn't designed as a lock picker, but he could use it that way.

It took less than ten seconds to electronically retract the bolt. As soon as he threw open the door, the dials on the instrument in his hand went haywire. Something inside the house was generating a powerful electromagnetic pulse.

He knew what it was. His eyes swung to the black box on the floor beside Jo. Guilt drove all shreds of common sense from his mind. When he took a step forward, readings on the meter doubled. At the same time, a wave of nausea swept over him, and he struggled to stay on his feet. It took all his remaining strength to struggle backward out of the field. When he reached the door, his head stopped spinning.

The box was small. It couldn't affect a very large area. From the door he calculated the distance to where Jo lay sprawled in the living room. Only eight feet, but it might as well have been eight miles. If he got any closer, he'd crumple before he reached her.

But he had to get her out of there. Before she— His brain wouldn't let him finish the thought.

Was there something he could use to shield his head? Wildly he looked around the porch and saw nothing that looked remotely useful. Then he spotted the garden hose still connected to the outside faucet. If his luck held, Jo hadn't gotten around to turning off the water for the winter.

When he opened the spigot, the hose stiffened and water spurted erratically from the nozzle. Tensely he waited to see if he was just getting leftover water from the pipes. Seconds later, he muttered silent thanks as the flow steadied.

Running back to the door, Cam adjusted the nozzle to produce a narrow stream and aimed at the box. When the force of the water struck the target, the box jumped as if it had been hit by a bullet. Water sprayed the room but the box was taking the brunt of the dousing. It sparked, crackled, and finally gave out a shuddering wheeze.

There was no other apparent change inside the room. But Cam checked the meter and saw that the room was now safe. Twisting the nozzle to shut off the water, he flung the hose onto the porch. Before it hit the wide boards, he was sprinting inside.

He knelt on the wet carpet beside Jo. *Not set to kill. Not set to kill.* The words were like a chant in his mind.

Gently he turned Jo over. For some reason, he was shocked to see that the rough fibers of the rug had pressed a pattern into the skin of her cheek. He was even more shocked by how deathly pale she looked.

With trembling fingers, he reached to find the pulse in her neck. Panic seized him when he couldn't find it. Finally he located the steady beat and breathed a sigh of relief.

At his touch, Jo stirred and moaned.

"It's all right. You're going to be all right," he murmured, praying that he spoke the truth. He didn't have much experience giving first aid. Or tending to unconscious females, for that matter, he thought, as he scooped her up and cradled her against the pleated front of his dress shirt. Even wearing a half-soaked robe, she was feather light in his arms. Under the bulky fabric her body felt fragile and very feminine.

Her color was returning.

"What?" she muttered, still not quite awake.

"You're all right," he repeated. This time he was pretty sure it was true.

He bent and pressed his cheek against hers. He was about to set her on the sofa when he saw that the cushions were wet.

Damn! Now that the immediate danger was passed, he could see that he'd made a mess of the place.

Still holding Jo in his arms, Cam turned toward the stairs. There was no problem figuring out which room was hers. The rest of the house leaned toward dark colors and sturdy furniture. The first bedroom on the right was an oasis of feminine warmth and country charm. The cabinet pieces were pine and oak including a carved armoire. Instead of a chest of drawers, there was a pie safe against the opposite wall. The curtains and chair cushions had been made from a matching blue and peach print.

Drawing back the antique quilt, he laid Jo on the four-poster bed. When he opened the front of the sopping robe, he forgot to breathe for a moment. She was wearing only a delicate bra and lacy panties that hid almost nothing.

He would have jerked the robe back in place except that his mission hadn't changed—he had to get her out of the soggy thing. When he tried to slip the garment from her arms, he didn't make much progress—probably because his fingers were now too clumsy to function properly.

Sitting down on the edge of the bed, he pulled her up and forward. But her body was boneless. She collapsed against him, the air whooshing out of her lungs.

As her head drooped against his shoulder, the air rushed out of his lungs as well. For a moment he couldn't move. He'd been fantasizing about her. Now he was held captive by the pressure of her breasts against his chest, the silky feel of her skin, and the wildflower scent of her hair.

His arm came up to cradle her body protectively against his. At that moment, she was so sweetly vulnerable that he felt as if his heart would burst if he didn't kiss her. Turning his head, he pressed his lips against the soft skin where her cheek merged into her hairline.

He was confused by the strength of his emotions. But he wasn't the kind of man who took advantage of unconscious women, he told himself firmly. Letting out an unsteady breath, he forced his attention back to the job at hand. He'd just removed one of her arms from a sleeve, when he heard her murmur.

"Coming home..."

"Jo. Thank God."

Her body jerked as if she'd just realized what was happening.

"What in the hell are you doing this time?" she demanded. Her words were slurred but the message was clear.

"Your robe is soaked. I have to get it off."

"Soaked." She shifted and seemed to become aware of the sodden fabric—and also the proximity of her body to his.

When she pushed away from him, he didn't try to hold her. "From the hose," he mumbled.

"I was out in the yard?" As she spoke she shrugged off the wet garment and pushed it onto the floor. For a moment she sat there as exposed as a butterfly newly emerged from its chrysalis, the scar on her arm still a vivid red. Then she snatched at the quilt and pulled it up to her chin.

"No." He managed.

"No, what?"

"You weren't in the yard."

"The box," she muttered, sinking back against the pillow.

Cam reached for her hand. "How do you feel?"

"Weak. Confused." Her fingers gripped his as if she could draw strength from him.

He fought the urge to take her in his arms again. "Do you think the box came from your escaped con?" he asked instead.

She shrugged. "I don't know. It was with the mail. There was a note from my neighbor saying he'd ordered it from a catalog. It's supposed to be an ultrasonic pest repeller."

"That thing's no pest repeller."

"What is it?"

He wished he hadn't been so emphatic. "I had to douse it with the hose to short the circuits."

"What is it?" she repeated.

He sighed. She wasn't going to be sidetracked so easily. "My guess is that it generates an electromagnetic pulse."

"Something like an electromagnetic field? I've heard of them."

"No. Something different."

"What?"

"A crowd control device, I think. I'll take it back to my lab and check it out."

Jo pressed her palm against her forehead as if the gesture would help her brain function. The box would be evidence if she decided to call the police. After what it had done to her, however, the thought of having it in the house made her cringe. What if it went off again?

"How did it make you feel?" he asked, as if he had read her mind.

"Sick. Shaky. Frightened. Gonzo headache."

"I'm sorry."

"It wasn't your fault."

She missed the culpable expression that flashed across his face and the way his gray eyes were squinted in momentary pain.

There were a lot of things he wanted to ask. But she was in no condition to come up with explanations. Besides, he couldn't start raising questions until he'd gotten some answers of his own. "I'm going to get you some aspirin."

"Okay. It's in the medicine cabinet. There's a glass on the sink."

As she watched his tuxedo-clad back disappear through the bedroom door, she remembered what he was doing here. They were supposed to be going to a party at his aunt's house.

Thank God he'd come to pick her up. If he hadn't, she'd still be lying in the living room with that thing microwaving her brain. The image sent a massive shudder through her body, and her mouth went as dry as chalk as she realized what a close call she'd had.

He was gone longer than it should have taken. Maybe he was giving her time to collect herself. When he handed her the glass, she took a gulp. Then, self-conscious, she swallowed the aspirin.

He sat down in the rocker by the window. "This room's nothing like the rest of the house. Did you redo it after your husband died?"

"We had our own bedrooms. I brought a lot of these things from western Maryland. My grandmother made the quilt. The pie safe was hers, too."

"You and Skip had separate bedrooms?"

"Yes. I—we—" She flushed.

"You don't have to explain anything to me."

"I don't want you to think we didn't—" God, she wondered, why was she fumbling around like this? It must be the aftereffects of the box. But that didn't explain why she cared what he thought. "He used to read until three or four in the morning. The light kept me awake." The explanation ended on a slightly defiant note. "Where are your glasses?" She changed the subject.

Now he was the one who looked slightly embarrassed. "I thought I'd wear contacts tonight."

"You didn't have to go to any special trouble on my account." She started to push herself out of bed, until she remembered she wasn't exactly dressed for company.

"The party. We're supposed to be at your aunt's house right now."

"I hardly think you're up to it."

"Yes, I am!" Even as she issued the protest, a wave of dizziness swept over her.

"I'll be downstairs. You get some sleep and we'll talk about it in a couple of hours."

Perhaps to forestall further argument, he got up, strode to the door, and turned off the light. She heard his footsteps on the stairs.

When she closed her eyes, she knew she didn't have a prayer of going to sleep. She'd been too confused to think straight. Now the implications of what had happened were starting to sink in. If the box wasn't a dog control device, then Mac hadn't sent it. Which meant it had come from someone else—someone who wanted to hurt her. Had they set the whole thing up? Had they scattered the trash in the first place? Was that why Mac hadn't heard any dogs barking?

Under the covers her body went rigid, and her heart began to thump. She could feel sweat beading on her upper lip.

She was in her own bed, but suddenly she felt like an animal in the forest—an animal being stalked by some unseen predator. Only it wasn't a beast coming after her through the underbrush. It was a person. Someone who was poking and prying into her life and using the knowledge to terrify her. He knew her neighbors. He knew where she shopped. What candy she liked. Did he also know what soap she used? What cold capsules? Was he going to empty them out and fill them with cyanide?

Stop it, she told herself. But she couldn't halt the awful speculations.

Who? The same person who'd been calling her on the phone? Eddie? Had he trashed her yard the night he'd escaped from prison? Or was it someone else?

If she kept on like this, she was going to unravel like the slashed sweater she'd thrown away earlier in the week. She wasn't going to let it happen.

Since childhood, Jo O'Malley had had more gumption than most full-grown men.

After her father had died in a logging accident, there hadn't been much money. Her mother had supported the family by clerking in the country store down the road. The five kids had pitched in to keep the garden going; her brothers had supplemented the family diet with small game they brought home from the surrounding countryside.

As a child Jo had learned to mend a pair of jeans or a pair of shoes on the old treadle machine in the dining room. At twelve, she had gotten a job after school working as a maid at one of the ski resorts that dotted the mountain area. In summer the operation switched to boating, fishing, riding and the like.

Jo had learned three things very quickly. She wasn't cut out to be a maid. There was more than money that sep-

arated her from the vacationers. And education was
going to be the key to a better life.

Teachers at the local high school had admired her determination and her ability and had tried to curb her
natural proclivity for getting into trouble. They'd helped
her win a scholarship to the University of Maryland. But
when Mom had been laid up after an automobile accident, the family had needed money. Jo had quit school
and gone looking for a job.

She hadn't counted on falling under the spell of Skip
O'Malley. Now she knew that part of the attraction had
been his age—and his ability to take charge. He became
the stable male influence she'd never had. And something in him had responded to this girl from the country
who had needed taking in hand. The relationship had
been good for both of them. She'd played Eliza Doolit-
tle to his Henry Higgins. But like Eliza, she'd outgrown
the student-mentor relationship and matured into her
own woman.

Now she pushed herself to the side of the bed and
swung her legs over the edge. For a moment she swayed
and had to steady herself against the nightstand. Then the
spasm passed.

Somehow she walked across the floor to the bathroom. Somehow she ran the shower and got under the
hot water. It seemed to have a restorative effect. Or perhaps it was a combination of the hot water and her determination to feel normal.

By the time she dried her hair for the second time that
evening she was feeling almost human. To compensate
for her still-pale complexion, she put on a bit more makeup than usual. Then she donned fresh underwear and
the dress she had planned to wear to the party.

When she came downstairs, Cam was stamping on the fifth towel that he'd used to blot the rug. It still wasn't dry, but it was a whole lot better.

Hearing a noise in the hall, he spun around in surprise. When he saw Jo standing in the doorway, his jaw dropped open.

"I guess you forgot your spot remover."

He smiled. "This is too big a job, anyway."

"Then let's go to the party," she suggested.

"But you can't—"

"You can take me home early if I give up the ghost. Come on. We're already late."

Chapter Six

"Maybe I should call a doctor. The aftereffects of that EMP may be worse than I assumed."

The woman who stood rebelliously in the entrance to the living room stiffened her spine. "Do I look like I need a doctor?"

Cam studied the pint-size figure of defiance. From the top of her red hair to the toes of her black leather pumps, she looked ready to take on Baltimore's best. And the parts in between were definitely worth a second look.

The aqua silk dress she was wearing did wonderful things for her eyes and skin. The soft folds of the material played hide-and-seek with the curves he'd become acquainted with upstairs.

If she realized how much she turned him on, she'd probably use it to her advantage, he told himself. Better to get out of here while the getting was good.

He sighed. "You win. Let's go."

She seemed surprised and perhaps a little disappointed that they weren't going to do battle over the issue. He turned away so she couldn't see his grin.

The women he had dated would have slipped a fur coat over the silk dress. Jo pulled a trench coat out of the closet. On her the belted style was flattering and gave her an air of mystery.

But after they'd gotten into the car, he knew she wasn't quite as recovered as she pretended by the way she leaned back in the padded leather seat and closed her eyes.

"I hope you don't mind if we make a quick stop."

"Why?"

"Got to change my shirt. I was already dressed for the party when disaster struck."

"Oh—right."

The questions he wanted to ask about what had been happening to her hovered on the edge of his tongue. But he still didn't want Jo turning around with questions of her own, so he found a classical station and let the third Brandenburg Concerto fill the silence.

Cam pulled up in front of his Cross Keys town house.

"I'll be right back," he told her as he turned on a couple of lights and ushered her into the living room.

Jo melted into the comfortable cushions of an off-white couch and looked around with interest at the place where Cam lived. Even a girl from the mountains could see that the furnishings were very expensive. But the house certainly wasn't "decorated" in any high fashion sense, and it was a lot smaller than she would have expected. She didn't have much time to study the layout. As promised, Cam returned quickly. Then they were on their way to his aunt's nineteenth-century Mount Vernon residence.

As they ascended the steps, she fixed a smile on her face. When Abby Franklin greeted her inside the foyer with its fourteen-foot ceiling and carved mahogany woodwork, no one would have guessed that less than two hours before Jo had been flat out on her much more modest living room floor immobilized by EMP waves.

"I'm sorry we're late," she apologized to Cam's aunt. "But I had to see a new client just as I was getting ready to leave the office."

Cam watched the performance, amused and impressed with how well Jo handled the situation. Her claim might be true but it didn't begin to explain what had happened a few hours ago.

Steve came into the hall, and he and Jo hugged each other warmly.

"Making progress setting up your stateside air cargo business?" she asked.

"Sure am. Some of those contacts you gave me look like they're going to pan out."

The three of them discussed Steve's business plans for a few minutes. Cam was glad to see his friend sounding enthusiastic. He'd been worried about how a modern adventurer was going to fit into a more conventional lifestyle. Apparently he was finessing the situation. Was Abby as delighted with the arrangements? Perhaps she had decided it was better to have her husband flying around on this side of the world.

Steve clapped Cam on the back. "You and Jo are two of my favorite people. I hope you're getting along."

"Oh, we are."

Cam took her arm and they moved into the drawing room. Now that he'd gotten to know Jo better, he would characterize her behavior as watchful. What was she looking for, he wondered. And would her state of alert make it more difficult for him to take care of an important piece of business? Was she watching him as well as everyone else?

Just after the sit-down dinner for fifty, he got his chance. One of his aunt's friends had gotten into a gardening discussion with Jo, and they were exchanging tips on dividing irises and the best compost mix.

Quickly he slipped away from the group and made his way up the curved Georgian staircase. In the guest bedroom he quietly closed the heavy paneled door. Then he picked up the phone and dialed the familiar number he'd been waiting all evening to call.

BY TEN-THIRTY Jo knew that she couldn't keep up the game much longer. She'd wanted to go to the party to prove to herself and to Cam that she was functioning normally despite her mishap earlier in the evening. She'd also decided it would be foolish to give up the chance to check out the guests.

A whole bunch of nasty things had started right after the last party. If they weren't the work of Eddie Cahill, then perhaps there was a connection with the circle of Franklin-Claiborne-Randolph friends. Much as she hated to entertain the possibility, she couldn't dismiss it. So she spent the evening gliding through the authentically decorated Georgian rooms getting to know people.

Last week she'd felt out of place in the society crowd. Once she'd decided to employ her detective skills on her own behalf, she found that she was no longer feeling at a disadvantage.

However, as she chatted with Abby's cousin Glen Porter, she found her attention wandering. He was about her age and had worked as an extra in a couple of the recent movie productions set in Baltimore. She must be in bad shape, however, if she was having trouble focusing on his stories about Tom Selleck on the job. The aftereffects of the box were finally catching up with her, she conceded.

As if Cam had tapped into her thoughts, he appeared at her side, her coat draped over his arm.

"I have an early day tomorrow. I hope you don't mind if we make our excuses."

"I can give her a ride if you want to go ahead and leave," Glen offered.

Cam's expression took on a look of male possessiveness.

"No, I'm ready to go home," Jo broke in, strangely pleased by her escort's sudden show of covetousness.

PRISON TAUGHT YOU patience, Eddie Cahill thought. If you planned a job down to the last detail and waited for the right moment before you struck, you were sure of success. He'd already had a busy evening. Now he was waiting in the shadows when the flashy Buick pulled up in front of his ex-mother-in-law's house. He'd staked out the place before—as well as most of Karen's other haunts. In a day or two, he'd be ready to grab her.

The car had pulled up under a streetlight, and the driver cut the engine. Eddie wanted to stride across the cracked pavement and wrench the door open. Instead he pressed farther back into the darkness of the narrow alley. His stomach twisted as he watched Karen say goodnight to her new lover boy.

It hadn't taken sweet little Karen long to replace him, Eddie thought. While he'd been rotting in prison, she'd worked her way through a series of guys with flashy cars and money to burn. They all liked to walk into a restaurant or a club with a drop-dead, good-looking blonde on their arm.

The observation brought a mirthless laugh to his lips. When he finished with her, she wasn't going to be beautiful anymore. But she was definitely going to be dead.

Then after he took care of her, he was going to switch his full attention to that other bitch—Jo O'Malley.

CAM DIDN'T SPEAK until they were settled in his luxury sports car once more. "Maybe I was out of line. Did you want Glen to take you home?"

"Of course not."

She saw his hands relax on the wheel.

"How are you feeling? I was sure you were going to fold before the main course. You must be Superwoman."

Jo mustered a laugh. "And I thought I was out with Superman."

Cam looked startled.

"Hasn't anyone ever mentioned you look like Christopher Reeve?"

"No one else would dare." He turned onto Charles Street. For several minutes they rode in silence. "One thing about you, Jo O'Malley, I never know what to expect."

"A detective has to keep the opposition off balance."

"Do you consider me the opposition?"

"I guess I did at first."

"Why?"

"Your family probably served wine with dinner. Mine was lucky if we had root beer."

"So?"

"It's funny about the upper class. They take things as simple as food on the table or indoor plumbing for granted." In the dark, Jo worried a thumbnail between her teeth. She hadn't planned to dump her insecurities in Cam's lap. Now her tongue was flapping like a hound's ears.

Up ahead a traffic light flashed red, and Cam downshifted to a halt. "It sounds like you had a rough childhood."

"Rural poverty builds character."

"I guess that's true—if you're an example."

"What do you mean?"

"Don't you know you're an extraordinary woman?"

"Extraordinary? I'm just a simple country girl trying to survive in the big city."

"In my experience, most women fish for compliments. I try to give you one, and you throw it back in my face."

"A sexist compliment. That's a new twist."

"I hadn't thought about it that way." There was the hint of a grin in his voice.

Jo slid him a sidewise glance. A few minutes ago she'd thought she was too exhausted to put together a coherent sentence. Now she realized the conversation with Cam was having a stimulating effect. She suspected the reaction wasn't one-sided.

When they pulled up in front of her house, Cam cut the engine.

"You know, most guys don't care whether you have a thought in your brain," Jo said, turning his observation around on him as he escorted her to the porch. "They're more interested in figuring out how to make a move on you."

There was a long silence. "I'm not going to pretend I haven't had some thoughts along those lines. Does that bother you?"

Jo had been inserting her key in the lock when his words sank in.

"Yes...no."

The air around them was suddenly crackling with tension as though someone was beaming an entirely different EMP charge in their direction.

Superman moved quickly when he set his mind to it. Cam turned the key, whisked them both inside, and entered the security code that turned off the alarm system before Jo could blink. Then he was pulling her into his arms.

He'd been spinning fantasies about Jo O'Malley all week. Now, as his lips slanted over hers, he tried to hang on to the tattered shreds of his reason. He told himself he was conducting a scientific experiment. She couldn't possibly be as exciting as the daydreams that had been interfering with his work, and he was going to prove it.

Cameron Randolph had never been all that aggressive with women. When he'd been a kid in high school, the football stars—not the science fair winners—had made it big with the girls. After a couple of major disappointments, he'd told himself there were more important things in life than scoring. The tables had turned in college. In the right circles, intellectual prowess was a sexual stimulus. Being a good catch didn't exactly hurt, either. Without much real effort on his part, he'd found himself in the enviable position of picking and choosing the women who spent a few weeks or a few months in his bed. None of them had lasted very long, because none of them had claimed as much of his interest as his current lab experiments.

Things hadn't changed a lot in adulthood—even during the six months when he'd been engaged.

But now he held a woman in his arms who didn't give a damn about his money and who was a billion times more exciting than anything his fevered brain had invented. At odd moments all evening, he'd been torturing himself with mental pictures of the way she'd looked in her lacy bra and panties. Each time he'd felt as if he'd grabbed hold of a high voltage line.

His mouth moved over hers. Her lips parted on a bare whisper of a sigh. She was as warm as biscuits fresh from the oven. As sweet as homemade strawberry jam. As rich as fresh churned butter. Suddenly he was starving for the unaccustomed luxury of downhome cooking.

Experiment be damned! He knew the moment his lips touched hers that he had only been kidding himself. There was nothing experimental about the urgency of his need to feel her mouth open for him, nothing analytical about the shudder of excitement that raced through his body when her tongue met his.

Jo had told herself right from the first that she and Cam Randolph didn't have a damn thing in common. They were worlds apart socially, philosophically, economically. If she'd been capable of coherent thought at this moment, she would have acknowledged that none of it mattered.

They were male and female locked in the grip of a force older than time. When she felt his body shudder, she answered with an involuntary tremor of her own.

His lips moved over hers, changing the angle, changing the pressure, changing everything between them.

He muttered low, sexy words deep in his throat. The syllables were almost obliterated by the primitive assault of his lips on hers.

When his hands skimmed down her back and found the curve of her hips, she automatically raised on tiptoes, her body seeking the masculine hardness that fit so perfectly with her feminine softness. It had been years since she'd felt this way. Perhaps she never had.

But she was seeking more than simply physical gratification. Warmth, closeness. All the things she'd told herself she didn't long for.

"Coming home," she murmured. That was how being in his arms felt.

He shifted her body so that his hands could cup her breasts. They were small—but firm and perfect. Earlier when he'd taken off her robe, he'd seen the shadows of her nipples drawn to taut peaks from the cold water. They were taut now—from the heat he and Jo were generating between them. Through silk and lace, his thumbs stroked across the swollen tips, drawing a little gasp from deep in her lungs.

He ached with the need to go on touching her, kissing her, making love to her.

Instead he dredged air into his own lungs. He hadn't meant to go this fast.

"Jo, I—"

"Cam—"

They stared at each other, dumbfounded that they had traveled so far and turbulently. It was just a kiss, wasn't it? No, it was much, much more. Suddenly neither of them knew how to cope with the implications.

Her fingers trailed across her own thoroughly kissed lips.

"I'd better leave. Are you going to be all right?" he asked.

She nodded.

"I'll call you tomorrow."

Fingers still pressed to her lips, she watched him close the front door behind him. Then she turned the lock. She stood there until long after he had driven away, her emotional equilibrium in tatters.

She'd known sexual satisfaction with Skip. She'd known love. She had never known this white-hot energy arcing between a man and a woman. The closest she'd come to this feeling, she thought with a little grin, was when Tommy Steel had slipped her some white lightning at a church social.

But she wasn't high on anything now except Cameron Randolph. Was it just the skill of his lovemaking? Even as she asked the question, she dismissed it. She'd dug a moat around herself after Skip had died. No one else had dared to stick his toe into the shark-infested waters. But Cam had waded right in and forged across the dangerous channel. He'd charged up the opposite bank and into the stronghold—sword drawn—ready to help her fight the dragons breathing fire down her neck.

She shook her head. She was doing it again, casting him in another super-hero role. Drifting down the hall, she was headed for the stairs when she noticed the answering machine light was on. Still slightly drunk from the aftereffects of the kiss, she pressed the button.

"Did you have a good time at Mrs. Randolph's party, angel face?" the frightening voice that had become so familiar asked.

Oh God, he'd been watching her again. Couldn't she make a move without his knowing?

Jo's euphoria metamorphosed into razor-sharp horror. She pressed her shoulders against the wall in an effort to remain on her feet.

"I'm surprised you went out this evening after your little taste of my power."

She fought to swallow her scream. But her knees gave up the struggle to hold her erect, and she slid down to the rug. It was still soggy. Instantly chilly water soaked through her silk dress. Her teeth began to chatter and her body started to shiver—as much from fear as from the cold.

"Now you know that when I turn the switch, you'll do anything I want you to." The observation was followed by the high-pitched laugh Jo had come to know and fear. Moments ago her skin had been soft and tingly from Cam's caresses. Now it crawled with the pressure of a thousand insect wings. Beating. Beating.

"I have a nice brass bed all ready for you. I'm looking at it now. I can picture your red hair against the white pillow, your silky skin waiting for my touch, your wrists and ankles strapped to the brass rails. You're going to get everything you deserve."

Jo gagged. Unable to take any more, she reached out and pushed the fast forward button on the machine. An electronic garble assaulted her ears. When it cut off, she saved the message.

Her fingers dug into the soggy fibers of the rug. It was something to grip, a fragile hold on reality. Helpless fear threatened to swamp her. She wouldn't let it.

"You bastard," she hissed through clenched teeth, breaking the spell. Ejecting the tape, she clenched the small plastic cassette in her hand.

"You've had your fun. But I'm going to get you. You're going to be damn sorry you ever messed with Jo O'Malley," she grated, thinking about the caller ID attachment that soon would guard her phone. Then she'd know who he was!

Pushing herself to her feet, she started for the stairs. Her foot was on the second tread when she stopped abruptly, all at once aware of exactly what Laughing Boy said. He'd told her he was the one who'd sent her the nasty little present this afternoon.

It could have killed her. Maybe that was what Eddie had in mind. If it was Eddie.

When he'd started with the phone calls, she'd doubted it was him because the revenge had seemed too tame. But he'd escalated from words to deeds. What was next?

Well, she wasn't going to wait around and find out. She was going to take control of the situation. First thing in the morning she'd call the police and tell them about the EMP attack. No. She'd better get the box back from Cam first or they'd never believe anything so far-fetched. But there were other things she could do, too. Eddie—Laughing Boy—whoever he was—had given her a big clue about his identity. That box must have come from somewhere. Cam had said it produced an electromagnetic pulse. She needed to find out what the devil EMP really was. Then she'd see who manufactured the units.

The next morning she called Cam, but he wasn't in his office. Disappointment warred with other emotions as she acknowledged that she was having a morning-after reaction to their kiss. Last night she'd been so wound up with Cam that Skip O'Malley had been completely wiped from her mind. Now she couldn't help feeling a bit guilty and disloyal.

Jo had planned to go straight to her office. But as she dumped her soggy robe in the dryer, she remembered the clothes she'd dropped at the cleaners six weeks ago. She'd better pick the outfit up before they got pitched.

One was an apricot cocktail dress she'd planned to wear to a couple of the parties. Another was a tweed suit she often wore for initial interviews with clients when she wanted to look professional.

On her way downtown, she stopped at the cleaners. "My pocketbook was stolen, and I don't have the ticket," she explained to the woman behind the counter. "But my name is Jo O'Malley, and I brought the items in last month."

The woman behind the counter checked her records. "Our files show that those were claimed."

"Are you sure?"

"The ticket receipt is here."

How could that be? She hadn't picked them up. "Do you remember who collected them?"

The woman shrugged. "It was three days ago. There have been hundreds of people in here since then."

"Was it one of your regular customers?" Jo persisted, unable to squash the tight feeling building in her chest. It was happening again. Another invasion into her life. Or maybe the guy who'd gotten her purse was going to sell her clothes for ready cash. Maybe it wasn't related to the other stuff at all. "Can I talk to your manager?"

"Sure."

The most Jo could get was a promise that if someone realized they had the wrong laundry, she'd be called. If not, her homeowner's insurance would pay for the loss. She should have felt relieved that she wasn't going to be out the couple of hundred dollars, but she couldn't shake the foreboding hovering over her.

Still, there was nothing more she could do about the missing clothes. And there were more pressing matters to take care of. Back at her office, she flipped through her Rolodex until she found the name of Harvey Cohen, Ph.D., past president of the Institute of Electronics and Electrical Engineers, former Princeton professor, and author of *The Electronic Warfare Game*, an exposé that had rocked the Pentagon a decade ago. Antiestablishment money had set him up in a Columbia, Maryland, think tank where he nipped at the heels of government agencies eager to spend public funds without regard for public health and safety.

Jo smiled as she conjured up a mental picture of Dr. Cohen. He'd been in the thick of the sixties radical movement. Thirty years later he still wore his curly hair in a halo around his face and favored cords and turtlenecks instead of suits. A suit would have hidden the little potbelly that spilled over his belt buckle.

Jo had met him a year ago when she'd done some undercover work aimed at stopping the Defense Department from filling in Eastern Shore wetland and building a weapons plant. They'd both been dressed as duck hunters that morning at dawn when she'd taken him out in a small boat to tour the area. He'd asked her to call him anytime she needed his help. She was still surprised when his secretary put her right through.

"Jo! Glad to hear from my favorite sneak boat pilot. I assume this isn't just a social call."

"Very astute, Professor. I'm wondering what you can tell me about EMP."

"As in Operation Sleeping Beauty?"

"If you say so."

"That's the code name for one of the government's secret research projects. I assume you don't want technical jargon."

"Right."

"In a nutshell, the Defense Department is very interested in using EMP to disrupt the functioning of the body's central nervous system. Actually it could be a very effective weapon against terrorists who have hijacked an airplane. Once they're on the ground, you zap the plane with EMP waves and everybody inside starts throwing up or goes temporarily blind and deaf or keels over. Or if you want to turn up the juice, you could use focused beams of high-powdered radio-frequency waves to kill by literally frying brain cells.''

Jo shivered. She'd felt as if her brain cells were being fried when the box had switched on. Obviously it hadn't been set to kill. Or she wouldn't be talking to Dr. Cohen.

''So it's all still experimental. Who's doing research in the field?''

''The Navy has a contract out. U.C.L.A. had something going at their Brain Research Institute.''

Jo could hear papers being shuffled on the other end of the line.

''Hmm—let's see—there was a local contract that never panned out. With Randolph Enterprises. Wonder boy Cameron Randolph was supposed to be working on a prototype for the Army.''

Chapter Seven

"Cameron Randolph?" Jo repeated carefully, hoping she'd heard Harvey Cohen wrong.

"Do you know young Randolph? Hell of an inventor."

Jo's mind tried to process the new information. "We've met," she managed.

"I'm a little vague on what happened with the EMP deal, but as I understand it, he reneged on the government contract. He paid back what they'd already given him plus a penalty, but there was some talk of suing him, anyway. I don't think it came to anything."

"Why did he renege?" It was hard to speak around the wad of cement that had wedged itself in her throat.

"The rumor was, he declined to test his prototype device on prisoner volunteers—said there was no way of knowing whether there were any permanent effects."

Jo realized that the hand gripping the receiver had turned clammy. Permanent damage. Did she have any permanent damage from that session with the box last night? Transferring the phone, she wiped her palm on her skirt.

"I can send you a summary of the current literature. You might want to take a look at an article in the I.E.E.E. Journal."

"Uh, thanks."

When Jo hung up, her heart was thumping around in her chest like a tennis shoe in a clothes dryer.

"Get a grip on yourself," she hissed between clenched teeth. "You've still got all your marbles." But her body simply wouldn't respond to the command. She wasn't just worried about her brain cells. Cam had lied to her last night. No, that wasn't exactly true. He'd simply forgotten to mention that he'd invented the device that had mowed her down like a field of tobacco in a hurricane.

What else had the man lied about? The possibilities were so hideous that her whole body turned clammy. Scary things had been happening to her ever since the engagement party for Abby. Last night she'd wondered if someone at the Franklin mansion was responsible. What if that someone were Cameron Randolph? The man who'd conveniently come along and rescued her. The man who'd made her feel as if Fourth of July fireworks were exploding in her body when he'd held her in his arms last night.

The phone rang, and she snatched the receiver from the cradle.

"Hello!" she barked.

"I was calling to find out how you were feeling. If I had to answer the question myself—I'd say belligerent."

"Cam."

"Jo, what's the matter?"

"Do you think you could come down to my office? I need to talk to you."

There was a long pause on the other end of the line. "Right now?"

"Yes."

"I'll be there in twenty minutes."

As she hung up the phone, Jo could hardly believe the brief conversation. The gut-wrenching need to confront Cam with her knowledge had banished any other considerations. She had to know what was going on. Now she wondered if she were stupidly putting herself in even more danger.

Opening her desk drawer, she made sure that the revolver she'd brought from home to replace the stolen one was loaded. Then she methodically began to clear the piles of folders and mail off her desk. She didn't make any attempt to sort the material. She simply swept it into stacks and set them on the floor of the closet. When the surface was clear, she pulled the two answering machine tapes from the middle drawer and placed them on the blotter. Then she positioned a tape recorder in front of them.

She had barely finished when a loud knock made her jump. Less than twenty minutes, she thought as she glanced up to see the male silhouette filling the rectangle of frosted glass. Had the man driven or had he flown through the air with his red cape streaming behind him? She got up and hurried across the room but stopped with her hand on the knob—suddenly remembering an important detail that had failed to penetrate her fogged brain last night. Cam had gotten into her house without battering down the door or breaking any windows.

What was she dealing with? Well, it was too late to change her mind now. If he wanted to get in, she couldn't stop him. When she flung the door open, they stared at each other. Jo was struck with a feeling of unreality. Friends? Strangers? Enemies? She didn't know. She couldn't trust her judgment.

As she backed away, he followed her inside and closed the door.

"What's bothering you?"

Jo circled around so that the large bulk of the desk was between them. Deliberately she sat down and positioned her hand near the desk drawer. Taking his cue from her, Cam pulled up one of the sturdy wooden armchairs.

Now that he wasn't looming over her, she was able to study his appearance. He looked as if he'd gone home, changed out of his tuxedo and spent the night in a pair of gray slacks and a white cotton shirt. They were both rumpled. And his lean face was haggard and unshaven.

"You tell me what's bothering *you*." She turned his question into a demand.

"Last night at my aunt's I called Phil Mercer to get some stuff ready for me at the lab. I've been up all night running tests on that box that had you down for the count—and going through Randolph Enterprises records."

"And?" she prompted.

His Adam's apple bobbed. "That box. Jo, I'm the one who invented it."

She had pictured the way they'd play this scene. It wasn't following the script.

"I had the feeling you weren't being straight with me yesterday. Why didn't you tell me the truth?"

"I wasn't one hundred percent sure of the facts."

"How did your invention end up in my living room?"

"I've been asking myself that question for hours."

The look of anguish on his face made Jo's chest squeeze painfully, but she met his gaze squarely, studying his features. In her profession, she'd encountered her share of accomplished liars. All were natural performers, outgoing, charming people—not introverted research scientists. Liars betrayed themselves in all sorts of little ways. Flashes of emotion that revealed their real feelings. Lopsided expressions that were slightly stronger on one side of the face than the other. None of the signs were evident. She was willing to stake her reputation on the certainty that Cameron Randolph wasn't lying to her.

Jo clutched the knowledge to her breast like a child clutching a security blanket in the middle of the night. However, she needed to know more if she were ever going to trust him again. It wasn't a question of staking her reputation. It was more like staking her life.

"I think you'd better tell me about it," she prompted.

"Do you want to know why I took the government contract in the first place? Or the part about how the damn invention slipped out of my control?"

"Why don't you start from the beginning?"

He pounded his fists against the chair arms. "God knows I didn't need the money. In fact, the damn project ended up *costing* Randolph Enterprises a hell of a lot. When I first started investigating the concept, the intellectual aspects of EMP research excited me. That's why I put in a bid in the first place. When it came down to conducting tests on prison volunteers, I realized I didn't want to take that kind of responsibility."

Jo nodded. Without any prompting on her part, he was confirming what Harvey Cohen had said. He went on to tell her about canceling the contract and paying back the money. Then he stopped abruptly. His teeth were clenched together, and his hands gripped the arms of the wooden office chair. Jo felt her own tension leaping up to match his.

When he began to speak again, his voice was as brittle as a batch of semiconductors plunged into a vat of liquid nitrogen.

"I thought I'd closed that chapter of my life—until I found you lying unconscious on your living-room rug. When I got the box back to the lab last night, I took it apart and checked the circuitry. Then I checked my specs on the project. I hadn't realized it before, but the EMP files must have been some of the ones that were copied from us several years ago."

"Copied?"

"As in industrial espionage. All the original records are still there. But the box is a perfect replica of my design—down to the casing. The only difference is that someone added a pressure trigger so it would switch on when the cardboard wrapping was removed." His gray eyes were hard. "We had some other plans stolen before my father died. A couple of prototypes I developed ended up being marketed by other companies."

"Who was stealing the plans?"

"We never found out."

"But the problem stopped?"

"Yes," he clipped out. "Jo, this is strictly confidential information."

"I understand."

Before she could ask him another question, he cut in with one of his own. "You didn't get me down here because you knew anything about the espionage, did you?"

"No."

He nodded, as if the answer satisfied some need of his own. Then he gestured toward the machine in the middle of the blotter. "Are you recording our conversation? Or did you want to play a tape for me?"

The ghost of a smile flickered around her lips. It vanished almost at once. "To play a tape. Cam, a lot of disturbing things have been happening to me lately. Not just the EMP stuff last night." Picking up one of the cassettes she inserted it into the recorder and pressed the button.

"You've got a gorgeous little body, angel face, you know that?" the electronically distorted voice began. Jo had heard it before and thought she was prepared. Still, her palms dampened and her skin began to crawl. She shot Cam a glance. His expression was grim.

"*This* is the call you got the other day?"

"Shh. Just listen."

". . . what I'd like to do to you makes me hot all over, baby. The problem is, I can't decide whether I want to give you a poke with my sugar stick or stick you with a hot poker."

Listening to that sort of smut in private was one thing. Now her cheeks heated as embarrassment overlaid her other reactions to the recording.

Cam muttered a curse. His expression had gone from grim to murderous.

"Get the wordplay? But when you and me play, baby, it ain't just gonna be with words."

"My God, Jo—" Cam began.

"There's more. Let me play the other one before I lose my nerve." Her hands were shaking now as she removed one tape and inserted the other one into the recorder.

"Did you have a good time at Mrs. Randolph's party, angel face?" the distorted electronic voice that had become a part of her life asked once again. Unconsciously Jo wedged her shoulders against the back of the chair the way she'd pressed them against the wall last night when she'd first heard the message, but she couldn't stop her whole body from trembling. Her hands were clenched. Her fingernails dug into the palms of her hands the way she'd dug into the fibers of the rug.

Cam was out of his seat and around the desk before the caller delivered his next line. Pulling Jo up, he took her in his arms. Then he lowered himself into the chair and cradled her in his lap.

"I'm surprised you went out this evening after your little taste of my power."

She felt Cam's body tense, heard him swear again.

"Now you know that when I turn the switch, you'll do anything I want you to. I have a nice brass bed all ready for you. I'm looking at it now. I can picture your red hair against the white pillow, your silky skin waiting for my touch, your wrists and ankles strapped to the brass rails. You're going to get everything you deserve."

She'd sworn listening to the tapes again with Cam wasn't going to knock the props out from under her. Somehow his arms around her shoulders and his chin pressed to the top of her head shattered her fragile hold on equanimity. She'd been dealing with this alone. Now her teeth began to chatter the way they had when she'd collapsed on the wet rug.

He rocked her gently, waiting for the attack of fear to pass. In his embrace, the trembling subsided.

"Cam, I tried to call you this morning. When I couldn't reach you, I did some checking on my own. I knew you had invented an EMP prototype."

His body jerked. "I can imagine what you must have concluded. At least you picked up the phone instead of a gun."

Perhaps because of the tension in the room, the observation made her a little giddy. Turning around, she pulled open the desk drawer. "I wasn't taking any chances. The gun's right in here."

He whistled through even white teeth. "I'm glad we're on the same side."

"Who are we fighting? Was Eddie Cahill ever in a position to get into Randolph Enterprises files?"

"Eddie Cahill. The escaped con you told me about at the party? Last night I was wondering if he might have sent you that box."

"Me, too."

"What does Cahill look like?"

"There's a picture in my file." Jo slid off Cam's lap, opened the closet door, and went down on her knees to go through the folders.

"You keep your files on the closet floor?"

"About every two weeks, I catch up with them."

She brought a stack of folders back to the desk. A few minutes later she handed Cam several photographs of Eddie Cahill.

He studied the man. Slight build. Medium-length brown hair. Black eyes that were both defiant and watchful. A scar on the right side of his upper lip. "He doesn't look familiar."

"He was vain about his haircuts. He's probably making death threats against the prison barber, too." Jo closed the folder.

"Did he make a death threat against you?"

"Not those exact words." Jo sank back into the chair opposite the desk. Succinctly she filled Cam in on the history of her association with the drug dealer—ending with his courtroom curse.

"He could be the one making the calls. Even if he didn't steal the EMP plans, he may know the person who did," Cam conceded. "Maybe he bought the box. Maybe they've become a new intimidation device among Baltimore's criminal element."

"I think I would have heard about it. Unless I'm a test case."

Cam worried his bottom lip between his teeth. "You've only received those two calls?"

"Three. One was live."

"The guy on those tapes knows a hell of a lot about you."

"Why do you think it's a guy?"

"Would a woman say those things?"

"I guess not." Now that they had begun to discuss the problem, Jo found herself wanting to share some of her insights. It was just like the old days, when she and Skip had hashed over one of their cases. "I was wondering last night if someone at the party was responsible—since everything started right after the reception at the Franklins'."

"So that's why you were playing social butterfly. You were looking for leads."

"Yes. Cam, what if it's not Eddie at all? What if it's somebody else?"

"But who?"

She shrugged. "Someone else with a grudge against me. I don't know."

"Have you talked to the police?"

"About Eddie. And I reported the mugging. I was going to tell them about the box—but you took it away."

He looked chagrined. "Have you told them about the calls?"

"I've talked to the phone company. I'm getting one of those new caller ID systems. That's going to solve the phone harassment problem. When I have the evidence, I'll take it to the police."

"Don't you think they ought to have the whole picture now?"

"What do you think they're going to do? Put a twenty-four-hour guard on me? They don't have the manpower, and even if they did, private detectives don't call the police every time they get an obscene phone call."

He swore vehemently. "Did Skip O'Malley teach you that claptrap?"

She sat up straighter in her chair. "Skip O'Malley was the best. He taught me everything I know."

"He got himself killed on a case, didn't he?"

"How do you know that?"

"I checked some back issues of the *Baltimore Sun*."

"Why?" she demanded.

"I wanted to know more about you," he pointed out reasonably.

"You could have asked."

"When I want facts, I go look them up. Isn't that what you did this morning when you checked up on me?"

She glared at him. "I didn't know that checking up on EMP was going to lead back to you."

"Why is it," he asked slowly, "that when the two of us seem to be getting closer, Skip O'Malley steps between us?"

"He was my husband."

"He's been dead for three years and you're still wearing his ring."

Her eyes went to the narrow gold band she'd transferred to her right hand. "What's wrong with that?"

"Jo, I understand why you're on edge. Anyone would be after getting those calls. I even understand why I represent some kind of threat to your loyalty to Skip. Last night when I kissed you, you weren't thinking about Skip O'Malley."

She'd admitted as much this morning. Somehow when he said it, her defensive shields went up. "Of all the colossal male arrogance."

"Okay. You're not ready to talk about it. I'll call you in a couple of days. Or if you need me—"

"What I need is for you to get out of my seat so I can get back to work."

He got up as if he'd just realized whose chair he had confiscated. Sheepishly he headed for the door. When he reached it, he hesitated.

Jo didn't call him back. Long after he'd left, she sat staring at the frosted glass of the door. Damn him, she thought. Damn him. He was right. He was the only man who'd made her insides melt in the three years since Skip had died.

But that didn't mean she hadn't made a big mistake.

OUT ON THE STREET, Cam folded his arms across his chest. When Jo had summoned him down here, she'd sounded so upset that he'd dashed out of the office without a coat. Earlier he hadn't even felt the November chill. Now he did.

He thought about surprising Jo by marching back into her office, taking her by the shoulders and shaking some sense into her. Then he was shocked by his caveman thoughts.

Instead of acting on the impulse, he walked briskly toward the garage where the Lotus was parked. When he'd reopened Skip O'Malley's investigation, he'd thought he'd understood his own motives. Now his stomach knotted as he grappled with confusion. He'd always prided himself on his rational, scientific powers. Well, his cool detachment had been shot to hell.

He cared about Jo. A lot. Unfortunately his new feelings were at war with his old loyalties. He still hadn't told her everything. Perhaps that wasn't fair. His stomach clenched tighter. What had happened in the past had hurt him. He couldn't just let go. If he did, he'd be letting go of part of his life. Somehow he had to make it all come out right.

Jo DELIBERATELY kept her mind off Cam. Instead she called Mrs. Douglas at the phone company again. The woman had already talked to her supervisor. "It's highly irregular to give out information about harassing calls," she repeated, and Jo was afraid she wasn't going to get the names. "But under the circumstances," she continued, "I've obtained permission."

"I appreciate that," Jo told her sincerely.

When she came down to the office, Mrs. Douglas handed a sheet of paper across the desk. Jo scanned the names, addresses and now-unlisted home numbers—along with work numbers. There were also notations of when the calls had been received. Some were almost three years ago. "Thanks."

"If you get a lead on the caller, I assume you'll share the information with us."

"Of course," Jo agreed. "Is there an office I can use?"

Mrs. Douglas led her down the hall to a cubicle with a modular desk and set of phones.

"This will be fine."

The first woman she tried wasn't home. The second, Melody Naylor, worked at the Hairsport—a unisex salon on Route 40. She wasn't able to talk on the phone because she was giving a customer a perm. When Jo persisted, she said if the detective could stop by in the next hour she wouldn't mind answering a few questions.

Melody turned out to be a petite blonde in her late twenties who was wearing blue jeans and a fringed cowgirl shirt. Two pairs of dangling gold earrings hung from her small lobes.

"Yeah, I did get a couple o' calls about eighteen months ago," she told Jo as she expertly rolled and clipped sections of hair. "But, see, I figured it was my ex-boyfriend. We'd just broken up, and he wasn't taking it very well."

"Did you ever get him to admit it?" Jo asked.

She shrugged. "He just laughed when I asked him."

Laughed, Jo thought. That could fit.

"He left town about the same time the calls stopped," Melody continued.

"Why did you make a report to the phone company if you thought you knew who it was?"

"The jerk was calling me at work and tying up the line."

Jo was about to ask another question when the shop door opened. The women who entered fixed Melody with a sharp look. "My manager," the hairdresser whispered. "I thought she was gonna be out longer."

Jo followed her gaze. "I could get back to you later."

"No. There isn't much else I can tell you. The whole thing's been over for a long time, and I'd rather forget it, anyway."

Jo left wishing she'd gotten more information. Back at the office, she tried phoning several other names on the list. One of the women had moved. Another didn't want to talk about the incident.

With progress like this, she might have the case solved in a couple of hundred years, Jo thought on a discouraged sigh. She was about to go home for the day when the UPS man knocked on the door. To Jo's delight, he'd brought the caller ID attachments for the phone. Now she had a much more productive way of attacking the problem.

As soon as the delivery man left, she hooked up one box at her office. She'd plug the other one in at home. Then when that bastard called back, she'd nail him—and she wouldn't have to bother with a bunch of dead-end interviews.

All through dinner, she kept glancing at the phone. For the first time in days, she hoped it would ring. But it didn't.

After she washed the dishes, she called Laura.

"Do you still want to help me set up that special photo equipment?" she asked her friend. Initially Jo had thought she might get a shot of marauding dogs. Now she wondered if she were on the trail of bigger game.

"Why not."

"Is Sunday morning still okay?" she asked, noting that Laura's enthusiasm didn't match her own.

"Uh-hum."

"If you want to get out of it, I'll understand."

"Sorry. It's not you. I'm just kind of down."

"Want to tell me about it?"

"I'll bend your ear on Sunday."

Saturday Jo rented rug and upholstery cleaning equipment and spent the day putting the living room back in order.

Sunday she skipped her usual breakfast. Despite getting the house back in shape, she was feeling a little depressed, and she suspected her friend's visit wasn't going to elevate her mood—since Laura hadn't sounded very chipper, either.

But when the blond lawyer knocked on the door, she had an upbeat expression on her face. The People section of the *Baltimore Sun* was tucked under her arm. She pulled it out and waved it aloft.

"Hey, you're famous."

"Famous?" Then Jo remembered the article about the Carpenters. She hadn't even brought in the paper that morning.

They spread the section on the kitchen table. The Carpenter story was the lead feature article. On the top of the first page were two photographs—one of the Carpenters as children and one of Jo's client as he looked now.

Jo scanned the text.

"This sure is going to call attention to the family," she said with a note of satisfaction.

"Bet it'll bring in some business for you. The whole second half is full of words of wisdom from Detective O'Malley."

"Yeah. I didn't think Sandy Peters was going to quote me so much."

"You're quotable. And it's interesting to hear about your methods."

"I didn't tell her all my tricks." Jo gestured toward the motion detector and camera, which were also on the kitchen table—along with a wooden birdhouse. She picked up the house and removed the roof. "I thought we'd put the camera in here, to protect it from the weather and prying eyes."

"Clever."

"We'll run the connecting wire along the fence and attach the motion detector to the underside of one of the horizontal supports."

Although Jo could have done the work herself, she was glad to have the company and hoped that Laura would open up about what was bothering her. After they had set the equipment up, they tested it by taking turns entering the line of fire. They got a picture of Jo mugging as she lifted the lid of a trash can and one of Laura with her hands over her face like a murder suspect ducking the media.

"You didn't really need me," Laura commented as she washed her hands at the sink. "Nobody needs me."

"Oh, come on."

"Well, Dr. William Avery certainly doesn't."

Jo spun around. "What do you mean?"

"He told me he wants a divorce. Yesterday he moved all his stuff out of the house."

"Sheez, Laura, I'm sorry."

"Maybe it's for the bes—" The sentence finished on a little sob. Jo wrapped her arms around her friend, and they stood in the middle of the kitchen for several moments.

"I promised myself I wasn't going to break down," Laura sniffed.

"Just let it out," Jo said softly.

Laura couldn't stop the bottled-up tears from flowing. But in a few minutes she had control of herself again. Jo handed her a tissue, and she blew her nose.

"You definitely think it's over?" Jo questioned.

"I found out he's been seeing a physical therapist from the clinic. When he moved out of our house, he moved in with her."

Jo snorted. "I can imagine what kind of physical therapy she's giving him."

Laura laughed. "Yeah. Let's see how she likes keeping his dinner warm when he doesn't come home till nine. Or listening to fascinating gall bladder surgery details when she's dead tired and has to get up at six-thirty in the morning."

Jo chimed in with a couple of ridiculous suggestions, and they both started to laugh. Then the conversation turned serious again.

"The scary part is worrying about making it on your own," Laura admitted. "I don't mean financially. I guess I mean emotionally. Not thinking of myself as part of a couple."

"I felt that way when Skip died. I'd come home at night and there would be things I wanted to talk to him about. It was hard getting used to the empty house." She didn't mention the way she felt now. She and Cam could have become a couple. That wasn't very likely anymore.

"I've had months to get used to that. Bill's hardly been around." Once Laura opened up, she spent the next hour talking about the marriage. Finally she sighed. "I don't know what got into me. It's a wonder you're still awake."

"You can talk to me anytime. That's what friends are for." Jo cast around for a way to lift Laura's spirits—and her own. "Hey. I've got an idea. There's a great Sunday brunch at the Hunt Valley Inn. Omelettes, Belgium waffles, the best coffee in Baltimore. I don't know about you, but I didn't eat breakfast this morning. What do you say?"

It didn't take too much persuading to get Laura to agree. They spent a pleasant couple of hours avoiding references to the men who were the source of their anxiety.

"Thanks," Laura said as she dropped Jo back at her house. "That was just what I needed."

After unlocking her door, Jo stopped to check the answering machine. When she saw there were several messages, her body went rigid. Then she reminded herself that the caller ID service was in place. If he'd called her again, she'd know where to find him.

First she checked the phone numbers. None were familiar, so she wrote them all down. Then, almost eagerly she pressed the Play button. No electronically distorted voice. No threats. Did the perp know she was ready for him? No, he wasn't clairvoyant, she told herself firmly.

The messages were all from people who'd read the article in the *Sun*. Two wanted to hire her. One had information he thought might be helpful in the Carpenter case.

The day had gone well, and Jo was in a better mood than before Laura had arrived. For dinner she microwaved herself a baked potato, slathered it with butter, and heaped it full of vegetables and cheese.

While she ate, she checked the cable schedule. She hadn't turned the TV on all week. But HBO was showing *Tin Men* again. Since she got a kick out of both Danny DeVito and the Baltimore locale, she decided to watch.

Just before eight she fixed herself a bowl of popcorn, changed into her most comfortable flannel gown, and settled down in bed. When she used the remote control to switch to HBO, the wrong movie flashed on the screen.

The scene made Jo cringe. It looked like one of those horror flicks where a guy with eight-inch steel fingernails chased a bunch of half-naked teenage girls around a high-school locker room before he started ripping out their throats.

Ten seconds of the mayhem made her gag, and she pressed the button to change the channel. The screen jumped for a second. Then the same scene snapped into focus. She pressed again. More gore.

With a muttered curse, Jo tossed the malfunctioning remote control onto the bed and marched over to the set.

Reaching out, she grasped the channel knob, and a jolt of electricity shot through her body.

A scream tore from her throat as she jumped back. Rubbing her hand, she felt the pain ebb. Her eyes were fixed on the television picture. It took a confused moment to realize what she was watching. Instead of a high-school locker room, the scene had switched to the deep woods. Now a group of teenage campers was being ripped apart by werewolves.

Squeezing her eyes shut, Jo gave her head a savage shake. That didn't shut out the screams of the victims. She was reaching for the volume control when she snatched her hand back. It tingled with remembered pain. She couldn't risk that again.

Her gaze dropped to the plug. Pulling on it could be just as dangerous as touching the controls.

Jo was backing away from the television set as if it were an alien when a flicker on the screen made her freeze in place. For a split second, the image had changed to something even more frightening.

Mouth dry and heart pounding, she held herself rigid watching the mayhem in the woods. Twenty seconds later, it happened again, and she gasped. A quick cut to another scene. She was left with the impression of a woman tied to a brass bed. A red-haired woman.

Jo's bare toes dug into the rag rug in front of the television set so hard that they started to cramp. But she couldn't tear her eyes away. The little insert flashed again and again on the screen—interspersed with a dismemberment in a sawmill. Hardly able to breathe, Jo viewed the next intrusion. Now she could see the back of a man as he advanced on the helpless woman. A knife was in his hand. Next time the image appeared, the knife arched down toward his victim.

Jo screamed and covered her eyes with her hands. Somehow that broke the spell. Snatching up the brass barrel-shaped piggy bank that sat on top of the pie safe, she flung it at the television. The screen exploded.

Chapter Eight

It should be over. It wasn't. Although the picture was gone, the sound remained. It was as if a demon had taken possession of the set.

Turning, Jo fled the room. Sheer black fright nipped at her heels. She hadn't realized that the volume on the TV had been steadily escalating. Wails and screams followed her down the stairs. No. The sound was actually getting louder the farther away she ran.

When she reached the living room, she came to a screeching halt. The television. She hadn't turned that one on. But the horror she'd fled in the bedroom confronted her anew. Now it was on a twenty-five-inch picture tube. The sawmill. The helpless victims. And the woman on the bed. Only now her body was cut and bleeding.

On a choked sob, Jo sagged against the doorjamb. Terrifying calls. The EMP waves. Now this. Someone was trying to reduce her to a quivering mass of fear. Her hands balled into fists. She wasn't going to let it happen.

The circuit-breaker box was down in the basement. She could turn off the sets that way. The cellar stairs were rough. Slivers of wood dug into Jo's feet as she pounded down to the utility room. When she snatched open the electrical box, she thanked God Skip had been much more organized than she. Each circuit was labeled. Furnace. Air conditioner. Refrigerator. Bathroom. Dining room. Living room. Bedroom.

Throat raw, breath hissing in and out of her lungs, she stood with her hand hovered above the last switch. A shock from the power box could kill. But if someone had wanted to electrocute her she'd be dead already, wouldn't she? Gritting her teeth, she threw back the circuit. Her hand throbbed, but only with the anticipation of pain. After the living-room switch, she flipped the one from the bedroom. The house was plunged into blessed silence.

Jo stood beside the circuit box, gasping. When she'd caught her breath she tiptoed back upstairs. The living room and the front hall were dark and silent. So was her bedroom.

Someone had gone to a lot of trouble to scare the stuffing out of her. Was it all Eddie Cahill's doing? Was this how he'd decided to punish her?

Had he rigged the television sets while she and Laura were at lunch? Was he in here now? Suddenly her scalp began to crawl, and she cringed into the shadows trying to make her body small and inconspicuous. Then she got a grip on herself.

She hadn't watched television since last Sunday. He could have done this anytime during the week. And if he'd wanted to spring out of the spare bedroom and attack her, why hadn't he already done it?

What if the phone and the EMP generator had been just the first and second acts of his private little melodrama starring Jo O'Malley. This was the third. What had he planned for the fourth? Tying her to the railroad tracks?

Or was it more like tying her to a brass bed and— All at once she knew she couldn't stay in the house straining to hear a lock turn or a window rattle. By the time she reached her darkened bedroom, she was limping. There must be splinters all over the bottoms of her feet, she realized. She couldn't do anything about that now. From the pie safe she snatched a pair of sweatpants and a shirt. The orange pants and the turquoise top didn't match, but she wasn't going to stop and coordinate her outfit. Then she grimaced as she yanked on socks and thrust her feet into loafers. The shoes made the splinters hurt all the more.

Despite the pain, Jo made it across the garage and into her car in two seconds flat. After locking the doors, she activated the opener and started the engine. Roaring out into the driveway, she paused only long enough to close the door again. Halfway down the street she remembered that she'd forgotten to reset the security alarm. But what difference did it make if he'd already been in her house?

Taking a deep breath she put her foot to the accelerator and sped off into the night. For the first few blocks, she kept one eye on the rearview mirror just in case somebody was following. To her intense relief, no set of headlights tailed her around the twisted course of streets through which she drove. She didn't realize until she'd found herself on Jones Falls Expressway that she was heading for Cam's.

She didn't even consider his reaction to the unexpected visit until she'd rung the bell. Then it was too late. Before she could think of exactly what she was going to say, he'd thrown open the door.

His eyes widened when he took in her disheveled appearance. "My God, Jo, what's happened now?"

"Well, my television has a big hole where the picture tube used to be."

He seemed to know she was starting with the least important detail. "You'd better come in and sit down," he said gently.

She followed him into the living room and flopped onto the couch. He sat down beside her looking uncertain.

Jo squeezed her eyes shut and struggled to get a grip on her emotions. Now that she was in the warm, sheltered environment of Cam's town house, she was afraid she was going to come apart.

"Do you want a cup of—uh—tea, or something stronger?"

"Something stronger."

Cam poured brandy into two snifters. While he stood at the bar in the corner, Jo willed the strands of her self-control to knit themselves back together.

When her host turned around, she was feeling a bit more composed. Yet she couldn't stop herself from gulping a swallow of the brandy. The unaccustomed fire in her throat made her cough. Cam waited patiently until the spasm subsided.

"Better?"

"I think so."

"Jo, are you going to tell me what really happened to you tonight?"

"Someone's trying to drive me nuts," she repeated the conclusion she'd come to earlier. "Or maybe the neighborhood Halloween committee is getting a jump on next year. When I turned on the television set tonight, all I could get was horror movies. When I tried to turn one off, it gave me a hell of a shock."

"Oh, honey." Before she finished the account, he'd crossed the two feet of space that separated them and folded her into his embrace. She didn't resist. In fact, she went almost limp in his arms.

His hands smoothed across her back. Her body absorbed the comfort. When she'd seen him last, they'd both been on edge with each other. Now it was as if the angry words had never been spoken.

"Not just regular horror movies." She swallowed low and slowly. "Interspersed with the commercial stuff was another scene. I could only see it in flashes. This guy had a woman tied to a brass bed. She was small, and she had red hair. I guess she looked a lot like me. He came at her with a knife. And he—and he—" Jo wasn't able to continue.

Cam gave her a few minutes to collect herself. "Tell me everything, honey," he finally murmured. "Everything that's happened to you."

"You know a lot of it."

"I want to understand the whole picture."

Jo gulped. "All right."

It felt surprisingly good to say it all. The longer she went on, the more convinced she was that everything fit into a pattern. While she talked, Cam held her close and stroked her back and shoulders.

"What do you think he's going to do next?" Jo finally asked the question that had been preying on her mind since she'd fled her house.

"I don't know. But one thing's for sure," Cam muttered, "you're not spending the night at home."

She nodded.

"And you're going to call the police and have them meet you over there so they can check this out."

"I already decided that."

Fifteen minutes later, they were heading back to Jo's. When the Lotus turned the corner onto her block, neither she nor Cam paid any attention to the van parked under the branches of a maple tree. Instead Jo's eyes were focused on her home. It was a strange experience viewing her house from the curb. Although it was after midnight, most of the lights were on because she'd flipped every switch she could reach as she'd fled the shrieks and cries blaring from the upstairs television set.

Jo stared at the windows as she climbed out of the car. Something wasn't right. Something— Then it hit her. She'd thrown the circuit breakers that shut off the electricity in the living room and her bedroom. Now the lights of both rooms blazed as brightly as those in the rest of the house.

"Cam! The lights. In my bedroom and the living room."

He'd listened intently to her earlier narration of events. Now his mind quickly followed her train of thought. His feet were already pounding toward the porch. "Stay out here," he ordered.

Ignoring the shouted command, Jo followed him down the front walk and up the steps.

He had halted at the front door. This time he hadn't come prepared with his lock picker. Jo produced the key. As soon as the door was open, they rushed inside. The living room was empty. Upstairs, floorboards creaked in rapid succession.

Cam took the stairs two at a time. Despite the pain from the splinters in her feet, Jo charged right after him. As Cam reached the second floor, he was greeted by the sound of shattering glass.

Something heavy hit the porch roof. By the time Jo made it into her bedroom, Cam was out on the roof. Jo was about to climb out when he came back into the room.

"Damn! He was out of here before I got upstairs. I couldn't even see where he went. If he broke in, I wonder why the security alarm wasn't blaring when we pulled up."

Jo looked down at her toes. "I, uh, forgot to reset it when I left."

Outside a car engine started with a grinding noise. They couldn't see the vehicle. But they heard it speed away into the darkness.

"He was here. Now I know the bastard was right here!" Jo spat out. She stared around her bedroom. The armoire was open. So was the pie safe. Along with the broken glass from the television picture tube, clothes were strewn around the floor.

"But I think he wasn't here long—because he'd only gotten to the clothes." She hobbled across the room and sank onto the bed.

Cam noticed the limp she'd managed to hide when he was looking. "What's wrong with your feet?"

"Splinters. From when I ran down the basement stairs."

A heavy pounding on the front door sent her springing to her feet, and she winced.

"That must be the police," Cam told her. "Too bad they didn't get here five minutes ago."

He went down to answer the door. Jo hobbled after him.

The officer who took the report was Detective Evan Hamill. He was a big man with ebony skin, close-cropped hair and a face that sported a two-inch scar across his chin. Jo had never met him but she knew the type. A fifteen-year veteran who had grown up in the inner city. When she told him about the bizarre episode with the television set, he looked surprised. But he pulled out a pad and pen and took a report.

"I guess this guy wasn't from the customer service department of ComCast Cable," Hamill quipped.

Jo gave him a weak smile. At least the man had a sense of humor.

"Can either of you give me a description?"

"No. He was gone before we made it upstairs," Cam said. He had found a pan and filled it with hot water. During the interview, Jo sat with her sweatpants pushed up to her calves and her feet submerged. The wet heat felt good, and she shot Cam a grateful look. He smiled encouragingly at her.

"It's not just what happened tonight," he said. "Ms. O'Malley has had problems over the last several weeks—ever since a man who she helped send to prison escaped."

That got Hamill's attention. "What's his name?"

"Eddie Cahill."

"Yeah I saw the report. He's one mean dude. And cagey. It looks like he started planning his escape the minute they slammed the gate behind him."

Hamill fumbled in his pockets. Jo expected him to pull out a pack of cigarettes. Instead he removed a bag of smokehouse almonds.

"You mind? I missed dinner."

"Go ahead."

With Cam's moral support, Jo forced herself to go through the story of Eddie Cahill, the phone calls, the mugging, the EMP, and the television sets again.

"It sounds like you're a target, all right," Hamill agreed, wiping his hand on his pants' leg.

"What kind of protection are you going to give her?" Cam asked, gesturing toward Jo.

"We don't have the manpower to keep someone with her twenty-four hours a day. About all we can do at this point is increase police visibility in the neighborhood and send more patrol cars past her house."

Jo shot Cam an "I told you so" look.

"I think it would be a good idea if she spent the night somewhere else," Hamill continued.

"That's already been arranged," Cam muttered.

"I want to have the lab dust for fingerprints in the morning. Why don't we make an appointment for ten."

"I'll have her back here by then," Cam told him.

When the detective had left, Jo closed her eyes. "Cam, I don't think I can face the mess in my room. But I need some stuff for tomorrow." She swallowed, wondering exactly what he thought she'd agreed to when she'd said she'd accepted his hospitality. "And a nightgown."

"Um-hum."

Their eyes locked for several heartbeats.

"I'll bring some stuff down."

"Thanks."

"Is there anything I can use to board up that window?"

"I think there's plywood in the basement. And my overnight bag should be in the top of my closet."

Half an hour later, for the second time that evening, Jo fled her own home. As she looked up at the plywood covering the bedroom window, she silently admitted to herself that she felt a whole lot better with Cameron Randolph next to her.

When they reached his Cross Keys town house, Cam opened the car door and swung Jo into his arms.

"I can walk," she protested.

"Your feet have taken enough punishment for one evening."

He set her down on the sofa where they'd first talked. "I'll be right back."

Jo nestled into the comfortable cushions.

When Cam returned, he was carrying a first-aid kit and a small lamp, which turned out to focus a narrow but powerful beam.

"We'd better get those splinters out before they get infected and you're really laid up."

"Yeah."

"Lie down."

When she'd complied, he sat down so that her feet were in his lap. Then he adjusted the beam of the lamp, swabbed her feet with a cotton ball soaked in antiseptic, and sterilized a needle and tweezers.

"That long soaking in hot water should help. But tell me if I hurt you." The tone was matter-of-fact, but the hand that grasped her ankle was amazingly gentle. So were the fingers that held the needle.

She peered up at Cam who was ministering to her as if they did this sort of thing all the time. A wave of warmth and gratitude swept over her. Out there in the night, someone had been stalking her. In here, she felt safe— and cherished.

Cam worked with precision, finding each splinter and easing it from her flesh with no more than a bad twinge or two each.

Several times he grasped one of her toes so that he could move one or the other foot to a different angle. There was a strange intimacy having him work on a part of her body that was usually covered up.

"I think that's the last of them," he finally announced. His voice told her that he felt the intimacy as much as she did.

Jo leaned back and closed her eyes. They blinked open again as cold antiseptic made her wince.

"Sorry."

"I don't think it can be helped."

Cam turned off the high-intensity lamp and set the first-aid supplies on the coffee table. But he made no move to get up. His hands continued to stroke Jo's ankles and to wander over her toes.

Now that the medical procedure was finished, she was free to enjoy his attentions. With one finger, he traced the arch of her foot, sending little shivers up her legs.

"Feet never turned me on before." Cam's voice was rough. "Did anyone ever tell you yours are damn sexy?"

"No."

He lifted one of her ankles, bringing her toes to his mouth. When he brushed his lips back and forth against the soft pads, Jo closed her eyes. When he started to nibble on them, she sucked in a surprised breath.

"Sorry," he repeated his earlier apology, quickly lowering the foot.

"That wasn't exactly a complaint. I didn't know feet were a turn-on, either."

When he'd brought her inside, she'd been exhausted and in pain. Now the air in the room had become erotically charged. They stared at each other for a long, breath-stopping moment. Then Jo held out her arms, and he came into them.

Stretching out beside her on the couch, he clasped her tightly. His lips skimmed along her jaw and over her cheeks before settling possessively over her mouth.

He kissed her for long, hungry minutes. She met each thrust of his tongue, each sensual movement of his lips with one of her own. When he finally lifted his head, they were both gasping for breath.

"Jo, honey. Oh Lord, Jo." He cradled her body against the length of his. "Friday when I left your office I told myself I wasn't going to call you again. I spent Saturday climbing the walls of my lab. Then tonight I called Steve because I needed to talk to someone who could give me a clue about how to handle you."

"How to handle me! What did he say?" She tried to pull away, but there wasn't much room to maneuver between his hard body and the sofa cushions.

"He told me to—uh—how can I put this politely— make love to you until you couldn't stand up."

"Sheez!"

Cam swallowed. "I'm not effectuating this very well."

"You and Steve Clairborne. I thought he was my friend."

"He is."

"He thinks sex is the quick fix for interpersonal relationships."

"No. If he did, he wouldn't have left Abby last spring and gone back to India."

Jo nodded slowly.

"He said he thinks you and I would be making a big mistake if we didn't give the relationship a chance. I think so, too."

Jo considered the words and the vulnerability she detected behind them. He had just offered her a chance to reject him.

She looked into his gray eyes, reading her own uncertainty but also an unspoken promise. Reaching out, she cupped Cam's face in her hands. "I think I keep littering the area with my emotional baggage. Then I get angry when you trip over it."

"Everybody has emotional baggage. If they've loved someone—and lost them. Or if they've been hurt by someone. Or if their childhood wasn't perfect."

"How do you know so much?"

"I'm smart."

"That's one of the things I like about you."

"What else?"

"I like the way you effectuate."

"Now you're making fun of me."

"I like the way you kiss, too."

"Gently or libidinously?"

"Every way." She relaxed in his arms once more.

Her words and the physical invitation drew him closer. He kissed her gently. He kissed her passionately. He kissed her tantalizingly. And while he kissed her, his hands began to move over her body.

His fingers slipped beneath her sweatshirt and inched upward. When his hand closed around her breast, the breath trickled out of her lungs.

They were lying on the couch facing each other. Ducking down, he caught the hem of the shirt with his teeth and edged it the rest of the way up. Then he began to caress her with his face and lips. "I could go mad from just tasting you."

When he began to tease one taut nipple with his tongue, a shaft of intense pleasure shot through her. She felt the madness, too, and her body arched into his.

Cam raised his head and looked into her eyes. "Could I interest you in a tour of the upstairs, starting with my bedroom?"

Jo grinned. "Yes, I think you could."

Pulling her shirt back into place, he helped her up.

Arm and arm they climbed the stairs. The light from the hall filtered into the master bedroom through the partly opened door. Cam folded down the covers on the king-size bed. Then he turned back to Jo. Between kisses and murmured endearments he stripped off her clothes. She did the same for him.

Naked in his bedroom. The reality was overwhelming. His body was lean and tough and very masculine. Tentatively she reached up to touch the dark mat of hair on his chest, feeling her fingers crinkle the curly hairs.

"Don't be shy with me, Jo. One of the things I like about you is that you're so direct."

She swallowed. "This is different."

"Jo O'Malley acting cautious. I never thought I'd see the day."

"Don't tease me."

"Honey, not holding you in my arms is teasing the hell out of myself." With a growl deep in his throat, he tugged her into his embrace, and they clung together.

When he lowered her to the mattress, it rocked gently.

"A water bed. I might get dizzy."

"Then you'll have to hold on tight."

She stared up at him as her arms circled his broad back, still half stunned just being here with him like this.

"I've fantasized about you naked in my bed," he murmured, echoing her thoughts. "I thought I was going to go crazy if I didn't make love to you."

Despite his statement, he didn't seem to be in a hurry. He enticed her with soul-searing kisses and tantalizing caresses until she was half out of her mind with need. And always he kept release just out of her reach.

But his body wasn't out of her reach. When her hand closed around him and began its own tender assault, she knew she'd tipped the balance.

She felt him shudder. "Jo, you're going to—"

"—have you inside me."

The hand that held him captive guided him into her body. They gazed into each other's eyes, acknowledging the moment's potency.

Then his hips began to move. He'd made a turbulent assault on her senses. Now he overwhelmed her with the power of a primitive male claiming his mate.

Her response was just as elemental. She moved with him, against him, around him, her fingers digging into his back as she reached the peak of sensation.

The tempest seized them both, racking their bodies with sensual spasms, sweeping away all reality but the two of them locked together in passionate fulfillment.

Little aftershocks of pleasure rippled over her as she nestled in his embrace.

He held her fiercely. Since the angry confrontation in her office, he'd come to realize that she was more important to him than what had happened in the past. Now there were things he had to tell her about his run-ins with Skip O'Malley.

Or maybe it was already too late for confessions. Maybe no matter what he said or did from now on, she was going to end up hating him.

No. There must be a way to keep it from happening. If she just got to know him better—to trust him—before she found out the truth, everything might be all right.

Chapter Nine

Out in the night, the man sitting in the driver's seat of the van banged his fists against the steering wheel. She was in there with that know-it-all, swell-headed Cameron Randolph.

Cam Randolph.

He'd taken her home so he could get into her pants.

A picture of the conceited inventor rolling on a bed with the little redhead leaped into his mind, and he spat out a stream of curses.

Once again, he got up and fiddled with the equipment in the van. With anyone else, he'd be able to hear what they were saying. Although probably they weren't communicating with anything more than sighs and groans.

He cursed again. Randolph must have some kind of electronic shielding around his town house. Just the way he had around his lab now.

The guy was a slow learner. But he'd finally caught on to the possibility that someone could be stealing his precious inventions.

In his spare time, he'd made a little study of Cam Randolph. The way he saw it, the lucky stiff had been born with the two big advantages in life—money and family. Sure he'd come up with some pretty good gadgets over the years. That didn't prove anything. Hadn't he gone to the best schools—gotten the best training money could buy. And he hadn't had to work for a living like everyone else. So he'd been able to shut himself up in his lab for as long as he wanted—until he'd gotten lucky a few times.

Everybody was always talking about how smart and how creative Cam Randolph was. Didn't they see the real reasons for his success? Didn't they understand what a cold-blooded bastard he was and that he never gave anyone else a chance?

FOR LONG MOMENTS Jo was content to just snuggle against Cam's chest, listening to his heart beat a strong, steady rhythm against her ear. "For years I told myself I didn't need this," she said softly. "You've changed my mind. But I never dreamed I'd get hooked up with anyone like you."

"You might say you have your hooks into me."

"That sounds painful."

"In a way it is. But then it's a new experience for me."

"You've never—"

"—cared enough about a woman to go after her like this."

Her eyebrows lifted.

"It's kind of nice to hold a woman in my arms who somewhere in the back of her mind isn't counting my money."

"Oh, come on. They've also got to be thinking that you're smart and good-looking and charming and a wonderful lover."

"Oh?"

The implications of her rash statement sank in. "You also have a habit of spouting big words when you're tense or embarrassed."

"I know. They're a kind of protective circumvallation."

They both laughed.

Jo was suddenly feeling better than she had in weeks. She nestled her head against Cam's shoulder, and he clasped her to his side. "When I was a kid in that shack in the mountains, I kept a stack of library books beside my bed. I went through everything I could get my hands on. My favorites were the Oz books and the Narnia books because they were about a magic place where some lucky children had gone to get away from the real world. I dreamed about doing that."

"I think I can understand why."

"One thing I learned when I got older—there's no point in sitting around daydreaming. You make your life what you want it to be." She swallowed. "Except that from time to time, Fate throws you a wild card. Like your husband gets killed. Or a psychotic decides he's going to show you slasher movies—and then come slash you to pieces."

His arms tightened around her. "He's not going to do that."

"It would be a damn bad thing, just when I've gotten my hooks into this brainy, charming, sexy guy."

"Jo." His mouth found hers again. And for a little while, they both shut out the danger waiting to envelop them.

WHEN THEY PULLED UP at Jo's front walk the next morning, a police car was already parked in the drive-way. Detective Hamill had arrived in a separate car, which was parked across the street. As they got out of the Lotus, he ambled around the side of the house. His jaw was working. More almonds, Jo thought.

"It looks as if the special TV programming was rigged through your cable hookup," he said.

"That was my hypothesis last night," Cam agreed. "But I didn't get a chance to check it out."

"By the way, what's the fancy photo setup out by the trash for?" the detective added.

"Photo setup?" Cam asked.

Jo explained to both of them, "I thought I was going to get a picture of some dogs. Maybe we got lucky last night." She went around back and checked the camera. The film hadn't advanced.

"Too bad," Cam said.

They all tromped back to the front porch, where Jo let the fingerprint crew inside. As they went upstairs to start in her bedroom, Jo headed straight for the living room. When she saw the answering machine was blinking, her body went rigid.

Cam was right behind her. "Let's find out who's left a message," he suggested in an even voice.

First Jo activated the recall mechanism on the caller ID unit. The number she wrote down definitely wasn't familiar.

Then she took a deep breath and pressed the Play button on the answering machine.

"Well, miss newspaper celebrity, I guess you think you're too important to have anything to do with me. I'm afraid you don't have a choice. How did you like the little movie show I set up for your personal viewing enjoyment?"

"He saw the article in the paper," Jo whispered, her skin growing clammy. God, she'd been a fool to put herself in the public eye like that. "I never should have let that reporter quote me."

Cam wrapped his arms around her and began to rub the goose bumps on her arms.

"That wasn't nice of you to bash in your television set like that. But I understand why you might have flipped out." The words were followed by one of his high-pitched laughs. Even the security of Cam's embrace couldn't stop the shudder from rippling over her skin.

"Easy, honey," he whispered.

She gave him a shaky little nod. This time she wasn't facing the voice and the threats alone.

"And it wasn't nice of you to go off with that slime-bag inventor," the voice continued on a harsher note. "Don't tell me you let him play bouncy bouncy with you. After that has-been Skip O'Malley, you need to develop better taste in men."

Jo's hands were balled into fists. With a look of helpless rage, she glanced around the room. "How dare he. How dare he," she gritted.

"He's just trying to get a rise out of you," Cam said. But he couldn't quite keep the anger out of his own voice.

When the message finished, Hamill pressed the Save button. "So that's the kind of trash you've been hearing," he muttered.

"I call him Laughing Boy," Jo told him.

"I can see why. Mind if I take the tape?"

She shook her head. "You can have the other ones, too. They're down at my office." Her fingers sought and found Cam's. His almost crushing grip was like a safety line.

Hamill was already dialing a special number at the phone company. In a brusque voice, he spoke into the receiver. A few minutes later, he swore. Slamming the phone back into the cradle, he turned to Jo and Cam. "It looks like we're not going to catch the bastard this morning."

"Why not?"

"He used a phone booth off Charles Street."

Solving the problem with something as simple as caller ID had been too much to hope for, Jo told herself. "He was here last night," she reminded the detective. "He must have seen the unit."

"Damn!" The exclamation came from Cam.

"If he called from a phone booth, how did he get that distortion in the transmission?" Hamill wondered aloud.

"Portable equipment?" Jo asked, her tone matter-of-fact now. She was going to think about this just like any other case. If she did that, the fear wouldn't swallow her up.

"I'd like to see what kind of setup he has," Cam mused. "EMP. Portable electronics equipment."

"Yeah." The police detective looked thoughtful.

"Do you think it's Eddie Cahill doing this?" Jo asked.

"I dug out the court records last night. You did some prime undercover work to nail Cahill. No wonder the mother said he was going to get you," Hamill answered. "But there's no hard evidence linking him to any of this."

"There's plenty of evidence that Ms. O'Malley's life is being torn apart." Cam looked toward the answering machine and back at Hamill. "Are you going to tell me you still can't commit yourself to protecting her?"

"I know you're worried—"

"Dammit, man."

"Cam, please," Jo whispered.

"I'll put everything I can into the investigation," Hamill promised. "And we've already increased patrols in the area. Basically Ms. O'Malley's doing the kinds of things I'd recommend. An alarm system. Good locks. Maybe she should put in some extra lighting in the yard,'' the police detective continued.

Then he turned to Jo. "Where can we reach you?"

"At my house," Cam answered.

She shot him a startled look. Helping her was one thing, making decisions for her was quite another. "Since when do you do the talking for me?"

"You sure can't stay here alone."

"I'm sure I'd be welcomed at my friend Laura's. She has a big house all to herself."

"Do you want to put your friend in danger?" Cam asked slowly.

"I—no."

Hamill cleared his throat. "I'd recommend taking Mr. Randolph up on his offer. He's likely to function as a deterrent. Whoever made the calls and rigged the TV stunt has been going after a woman living alone. He ran when Randolph discovered him in the house. He might give up if you had a protector."

Jo snorted.

Cam tried not to look victorious.

They waited until Hamill had left before continuing the personal discussion.

"I'm not going to spend the day hiding at your place," Jo informed Cam.

"What are you going to do?"

"I'm going to go back to those phone company records on other women who had similar calls and see if I can find out if they have anything in common with me."

"Would you mind if we stopped back at my place and had a look at your car? I'd like to check something out."

The question and his conciliatory tone of voice astonished her. "Cam, I'm not used to having a bodyguard."

"I know."

"I—things are moving so fast. I mean, with you and me."

"Honey, when this is over, I'll send you flowers and take you out to dinner at the Conservatory. Right now, I want to make sure you're going to be safe."

Jo nodded, unsure of how to act in this unfamiliar situation. "Okay," she agreed in a barely audible voice.

"Okay, we can go check out your car? Or you'll permit me to help you?"

"Okay to both."

Back at Cross Keys, Cam pulled into a parking place near Jo's Honda. She watched as he walked over to the car, stooped down and began to run his hands along the underside of the bumpers and under the chassis. When he reached a spot under the back bumper, he paused.

Seconds later he turned back to Jo. In the palm of his right hand lay a dull metal disk.

"What is it?"

"A directional transmitter. That's why he thought you were still at my house last night. He knew your car stayed."

Air wheezed out of Jo's lungs as the extent of her tormentor's scheme hit her. Her knees began to wobble and she sat down heavily on the curb. "He's been following me. Poking into my life. He's known where I was every second of the day and night because he's been tracking me."

"Yes." Cam was beside her, holding her.

"My God. What else has he been doing? If he's got a bunch of electronics stuff—he—he could have been listening to us." She gulped. "Like in your house last night."

"Not in my house! The place is shielded. Nothing gets in or out of that house without my knowing about it."

"Why?"

"I told you about the industrial espionage. Sometimes I take work home—or make business calls from there."

She nodded slowly and then raised an eyebrow in surprise as Cam got up and put the transmitter back where he'd found it.

"What are you doing?"

"I think we can lay a trap for the bastard." He worried a knuckle between his teeth. "Just let me think about how I want to set it up."

"Do me a favor. Let me help you think about it."

"Sure."

They drove in separate cars to 43 Light Street. While Jo waited in the back alley, Cam went down to talk to Lou Rossini. The building superintendent agreed to drive Jo's car to the vicinity of the pool hall where she'd been mugged. He'd take a cab back. Cam would park in a nearby alley and see who showed up at the car.

Before he left, Cam pulled Jo into his arms and gave her a hard kiss. "Remember, you're not going anywhere without letting somebody know about it," he reminded her.

"Yes, Mother." She wrinkled her nose. She didn't like having a bunch of constraints. On the other hand, the careful arrangements were comforting.

Sitting at her desk, she drummed her fingers against the wooden surface. She'd pinned her hopes on the caller ID equipment. It had done her as much good as a tissue paper dress in a rainstorm.

Now what? Maybe it was time to go back to the phone company list of women who'd been harassed.

Again she had to dial several numbers before getting anyone at home. The third woman she called answered the phone with the kind of cautious greeting that had crept into Jo's own voice recently.

"Is this Penny Wallace?"

"Who is this? How did you get this number?"

"My name is Jo O'Malley. I've been receiving some threatening phone calls. Since I'm a private detective, the phone company has given me permission to contact other women who might have been harassed by the same man."

"I really don't want to talk about it."

"Please. I'll only take a few minutes of your time."

"Are you the detective who was in that article in the paper Sunday?"

"Yes."

"What kind of calls have you been getting?"

"From someone with an electronically distorted voice." She kept her tone as steady as possible. "He seems to know a lot about me. And he's been leaving messages on my answering machines as well as speaking to me in person."

Penny made a choking sound. "That's what happened to me six months ago."

"Could I come over and talk to you?" Jo asked.

There was a long pause. "All right," the woman finally answered.

Jo got directions. When she hung up, she thought about the newspaper article again. The man stalking her had read it. So had Penny Wallace. On balance, the notoriety was probably more of an advantage than a disadvantage.

After locking the office, Jo went downstairs and started out the door toward the parking lot where she usually kept her car. Then she remembered the Honda was in Dundalk—and she'd promised Cam she'd stay at the office. Well, what Cam Randolph didn't know wasn't going to hurt him. Besides, this might be an important lead in the case. Going back inside, she called a cab and waited in the lobby until it arrived.

Penny Wallace lived in a redbrick row house in Catonsville. When she answered the door, the two women stared at each other in shock. They were both petite and both sported heads of short, curly red hair.

"You could be my sister," Penny said in amazement.

"That's just what I was thinking. Let's see if we can find out if we have anything else in common." Jo's voice brimmed with excitement. Finally she was getting somewhere.

Penny Wallace blew her nose and ushered her visitor into a small, neat living room decorated in a stark modern style. Well, taste in decor is something we don't share, Jo thought as she took off her coat and folded it beside her on the sofa.

"You're lucky you found me here. I've got a cold so I decided to stay home."

Jo sympathized before getting down to business. "When did the calls start?" she asked as she took a seat in a low-slung leather chair.

Penny faced her on the chrome-and-leather sofa with a box of tissues at her side. "May 15. I remember exactly because I'd just come home from Alice's wedding shower."

"You were in a wedding?" Jo asked carefully.

"I was the maid of honor."

The words sent a strange chill sweeping over Jo's skin as if an icy finger had reached out and touched her shoulder. "My calls started a couple of weeks ago when

I came back from an engagement party for one of my best friends. I'm the matron of honor in the wedding.''

Penny leaned forward. "That's spooky."

"Yeah."

"I know what you're going through. He's making sexual threats, isn't he? And he knows a lot about you."

"He knows everything about me."

"It was creepy. Especially the way he laughed."

"Yeah." Invisible insects buzzed around Jo for a moment. She willed them away.

"If it's any consolation, the calls stopped after the wedding."

"That's definitely something to look forward to. But I'm not just dealing with this on a personal level anymore. I'd really like to nail the guy if I can."

"I just wanted him to leave me alone," Penny whispered. It was apparent that talking about the episode had brought the whole thing back to her.

"Is there anything else that might help me track him down?"

"The music in the background. It sounded like a band."

"Yes! What about the stuff he threatened?"

"My therapist said the best thing I could do was put this out of my mind."

"I understand." Jo could empathize with that. "Did he just call? Or did you have any physical contact with him?"

"Just calls."

"Are you sure?" Jo gave a brief account of the electronic devices that had been used at her house.

Penny's eyes grew round. "Thank God I didn't have anything like that. It was all over the phone."

They talked for about fifteen minutes longer but Jo didn't get any more facts. "I wonder where he got the names of the wedding attendants," Penny mused.

"He could be a wedding photographer. He could work for the caterer or the florist. Do you know who provided those services for your friend?"

"No. I'm sorry. I could ask Alice and get back to you."

Jo gave Penny one of her cards and then asked if she could call a cab.

"A private detective without a car?"

"It's a long story."

Back at her office, Jo tried some more numbers and got another one of the victims, Heather Van Dyke, who was at home because she ran a sewing business from her recreation room. Now Jo had a better idea about what to ask. This woman, too, was a redhead within an inch of her height who'd been the matron of honor in her sister's wedding.

As Jo put down the phone, she leaned back in her chair. Two redheads and a blonde. How did that add up? Was Melody Naylor an unrelated case? She wished she'd asked the woman more questions.

Then a crucial fact flashed in her mind like the payoff light on a slot machine. Melody Naylor was a beautician. A lot of beauticians change their hair color the way other women change dresses. Maybe she had been a redhead when she'd gotten those calls.

When she phoned the shop, Melody was on a break.

Jo reintroduced herself and explained that she'd been talking to some other victims of phone harassment and might have discovered a common link. "Was your hair a different color when you were getting the calls?"

"Gee—let me think. I change it so much," the woman said, confirming Jo's speculation. "I was using Champagne Blond for a while. Then I decided to see if redheads have more fun, so I tried Fantastic Autumn."

"Your hair was red?" Jo clarified, her heart skipping a beat.

"Yeah. But I dyed it back just before Lucy's wedding because it didn't go with my pink dress."

"You were in a friend's wedding?" Jo asked, struggling to keep her voice steady.

"I was the maid of honor. And this real great-looking guy was one of the ushers. For a while I thought things were going t work out with us. Then he went back to his damn motorcycle racing."

Jo made appropriate responses as Melody prattled on about her love life. But her mind wasn't on the conversation. Redheads. Weddings. She touched her own red curls. She had the link between her and the other women. Could she find out why—and then who?

Chapter Ten

With renewed energy, Jo picked up the phone again. The next name on the list was a Margaret Clement. An older woman answered.

"Who's calling my daughter?" she asked in a strained voice.

Jo went through her now-familiar explanation, adding that she'd already talked to several other victims.

For long moments there was a silence on the other end of the line. "Margaret was getting calls like that," the woman finally said.

"Is she a redhead?"

"Yes,"

"Was she the maid or matron of honor in a wedding?"

"Yes. Her cousin's."

"Did the calls stop after the wedding?"

"No. They got worse. He was calling every day and saying such horrible things. And she started getting weird packages in the mail. One was a Christmas angel with red hair. Another was an electric bell that started buzzing when she opened it up." Jo's gasp was drowned out by the choked sob on the other end of the line. "Then Margaret disappeared."

Jo's fingers clenched the phone in a death grip.

"Back in August," Mrs. Clement continued. "She left her office to come home one afternoon, but she never got here. We haven't heard anything from her since."

"Could she have run away to escape the harassment?" Jo grasped at an explanation.

"She didn't take any of her clothes. And she didn't leave me a note or anything like that." Mrs. Clement's voice rose. "Margaret wouldn't have left me to worry like this. I just know she wouldn't. Besides, where would she have gone off to on her own?"

Jo had thought she understood the pattern that was developing. The new information and the anguish in the other woman's voice made her throat contract. "I'm sorry," she managed. "What did the police say?"

"They've been looking. So far nothing's turned up." The woman hesitated. "Did you say your name was Jo O'Malley? Didn't I read something about you in the Sunday paper?"

"Yes."

"I couldn't afford to pay you very much. But maybe you could help me find Margaret. She's such a good girl. Do you think he kidnapped her the way he said he was going to?"

"He made specific kidnapping threats?"

"Yes."

Jo shuddered. "I'm investigating the man, Mrs. Clement. I'll do what I can. Would it be all right if I came out and talked to you in the next few days?"

"Just call and let me know when you want to come."

Jo put down the phone. Her mouth went dry as she considered the new evidence. She'd been operating under certain assumptions. What if— She was saved from further speculation by a knock on the door. Her head jerked up, and she recognized Abby through the frosted glass.

"What's new?" she asked as Jo unlocked the door.

"Did Cam send you down here to check up on me?"

"Yes. It sounds as if you had quite an evening."

"And Cam told you all about it."

"Of course he did. Sweetie, the man has fallen hard for you. He can't keep from worrying himself sick over what's happening. Do you really blame him for that?"

"No," Jo admitted.

"You're under a lot of stress right now." Abby switched the focus of the conversation. "I'd say it's partly from the harassment and partly because you told yourself no one could take Skip's place—but you're beginning to wonder what a long-term relationship with Cam would be like."

Jo hadn't planned to discuss Cam. Now a sort of confession came tumbling out. "Last night, when he took me home, we made love. It was good, Abby." Jo's voice softened. "Not just good, better than . . . anything I can remember." The end of the sentence was as revealing for what it didn't say as for the actual words.

Abby crossed the room and put her arms around Jo's shoulder. "You're feeling guilty because being with Cam was warm and satisfying and made you feel cherished."

"How do you know it was like that?"

"I've gotten to know Cam Randolph over the past few months. At first I was sad for him because I thought here's a great guy, with so much to give the right woman—only he'd never found her. Then I started wondering if the right woman might be you."

"So you set things up."

"Not exactly. Steve wanted Cam for his best man. I wanted you for my matron of honor. But let's not get sidetracked from the real issue—your feelings."

"We sure wouldn't want to do that, Dr. Franklin."

"If you were in therapy, I'd make you work through things. But you're not. Jo, I've known you for a long time. I understand how you felt about Skip and what you went through when he died. You don't have anything to feel guilty about now. It's not a question of Cam's taking anyone else's place. It's a question of opening yourself to the possibilities of a new relationship."

"What about all the questions of money and social class? That kind of stuff. I mean, we hardly—"

"If Cameron Randolph had wanted a society girl, believe me he'd have one."

Jo nodded slowly. "You've given me a lot to think about."

"Good."

"Can we talk about my other problem? Unfortunately it's just as pressing."

"Fire away."

"I need some insights into the psychological profile of a guy who goes after redheaded maids of honor."

"Cam didn't say anything about that."

"He doesn't know yet. I finally made a breakthrough with the list of women I got from the telephone company. One of them let me come over and interview her. Abby, it was spooky how much she looked like me. And she'd been the maid of honor in a wedding." Jo went on to summarize the rest of what she'd learned, including the conversation with Margaret Clement's mother.

Abby looked alarmed. "That doesn't fit the usual pattern of a phone harasser."

"Or of a guy that was in the state pen until a couple of weeks ago—not when the records I have from the phone company go back two or three years."

"How do you think the wedding angle figures in?" Abby asked.

"Well, I'm not the psychologist here. But if I had to make a quick guess off the top of my head, I'd say that a redheaded woman rejected the guy who's been calling and maybe married someone else, and now he's getting even."

"And the caller is the same one who hit you with the EMP box and rigged your television sets."

"He told me he was."

"Oh, Jo. I hate to think that being in my wedding is putting you in danger."

"We still don't know for sure what's going on. Maybe Eddie knows about the wedding guy and is imitating his M.O."

Abby looked doubtful.

"Do you have any thoughts on handling the creep if he shows up in person?"

"I could tell you more if I heard the tapes."

"Two of them are still in my desk drawer." Jo pulled them out and popped one into the recorder. As she played the messages for Abby, she gritted her teeth and tried to evaluate them in light of the conversations she'd had with the psychologist.

"That man is seriously disturbed. He's not just trying to get a rise out of you with the sexual content. He's trying to terrorize you," Abby whispered when the second message had run its course.

"He's doing a pretty good job. What do you—uh—think about that brass bed? Didn't he make it sound kind of like a sacrificial altar?"

"That's stretching things."

Before she lost her nerve, Jo forced herself to spell out the terrible thoughts that had been in the back of her mind since she'd talked to Mrs. Clements. "He didn't just tell me about it. You know, I'm pretty sure that's what was flashing on the TV screen last night. Quick glimpses of a woman who looked a lot like me. Strapped down and helpless. In the early scenes she was wearing a long, white dress, then she was naked. I—I keep thinking," Jo gulped and made herself continue. "Maybe it was Margaret Clement. Maybe he was actually going through some kind of ritual murder with her. And he filmed it."

Abby's face had drained of color. She stared at her friend. "Oh, Jo—"

"I could be right, couldn't I?"

Abby nodded slowly.

"So if I end up in his clutches, it would probably be a good idea to stay off that bed."

"You're not going to end up in his clutches."

"What if I do—"

"Yes. Stay away from the bed."

BY THE TIME Detective Hamill came to collect the tapes, Jo was in control of her emotions. As if she were talking about any old investigation, she filled him in on what she'd discovered.

He was impressed with her detective work. "We could use you downtown."

"Don't count on it."

"I'll go back and pull the files on those cases to see how it fits in with the Eddie Cahill stuff."

"I'll get the names of the caterers and other service people each of the wedding parties used. Maybe there will be a name or address from their employee lists that will be some kind of link."

"And we'll keep each other up-to-date on our progress," Hamill added.

By the time Cam called at four to say he was coming back, Jo was deep into information gathering. She hadn't found out anything startling. But doing the work gave her the feeling that she was accomplishing something.

When Cam explained in a disgusted voice that the stakeout hadn't turned up anything, she was quick to reassure him that the idea had been worth trying.

"I debugged your Honda," he said, when he came into the office. "Then I put the transmitter in the garage across the street and stashed your car at Abby's apartment building." He stopped abruptly before continuing in a less confident voice. "If you wanted, you could see how Laura feels about a houseguest. I mean, if we made sure you weren't being followed, there wouldn't be any way he'd know you were there."

Cam wasn't pressing. He was giving her choices. That and the conversation she'd had with Abby tipped the balance.

Jo closed the file she'd been trying to make some notes in. "I'd rather go home with you," she said.

"I was hoping you would. Do you want to stop at your house and get some more clothes?"

For tomorrow or the next couple of weeks, Jo wondered.

As they drove up Charles Street, she told him about her new discoveries. His head snapped toward her when she came to the part about the redheads and the bridesmaids. "So maybe this isn't what we thought at all."

"I don't know how the new stuff fits in." Unconsciously she pulled her trench coat more tightly around her slender body, as if the fabric could protect her from more than the elements. "Do you think it's possible that two different people are involved?"

"God, Jo. I hope not."

"Then what?"

"We'll figure it out. Meanwhile, we'll keep you safe."

At her house she breathed silent thanks when she saw that the answering machine didn't have any messages. Then her mind reevaluated the implications. Laughing Boy knew everything else. Maybe he hadn't called because he knew she wasn't going to be home.

Wanting to spend as little time in the house as possible, she grabbed some clothes out of the closet and raided a few drawers. Then Cam was ushering her back out to the car.

He didn't drive straight to his place, and she knew he was making sure they weren't being followed. The way he handled the Lotus, only a stunt driver could have kept up with him.

Fifteen minutes later they pulled up in front of his door. Knowing that Cam's house was protected by every security device that was on the market or still in the development stages gave Jo a profound sense of well-being. Or maybe it was just being with Cam.

She wondered if he was feeling something similar. Once he'd closed the front door, he pulled her into his arms. At first it was enough to simply hold each other close. But as they stood in the hall, the feeling of comfort escalated quickly into sexual awareness.

They exchanged hot, hungry kisses. His hands were tracking up her back when they stopped abruptly. "When I get you in my arms, it's hard to remember about more mundane things."

"Like what?"

"Dinner, for instance."

"Oh, yeah. Dinner."

"I've got steaks, stuffed potatoes and green beans in the refrigerator," he told her. "So we don't have to go out to the store."

"Steak and potatoes," she said in a slightly dazed voice as she followed him down the hall to the kitchen.

Jo fixed the vegetables while Cam put the steaks on an indoor grill.

"We'll eat in the den," he said as he began to put plates and cutlery on a large tray.

He led the way into a comfortable room with sofas, a fireplace, and a thick shaggy rug. To her surprise, he set the food on a glass coffee table and pulled pillows off the couch. Then he used the built-in gas jets to start the wood in the fireplace. The dry logs were blazing in moments.

"Neat trick," Jo observed as he turned off the gas and let the wood take over. She wondered if she'd ever get used to that kind of casual luxury.

"I wish I had invented it," Cam remarked half seriously.

Jo, who had forgotten to eat lunch, tackled the food. "You grill a mean steak, Randolph. You're handier in the kitchen than you'd let on," she observed.

"It's just a basic bachelor skill."

"Before I married Skip he survived on meatball subs and frozen entrées. Then when we used to come home from work together, I was the one who had to get dinner on the table."

"Did you resent having to do all the cooking?"

"No. I grew up in a family that was pretty traditional. The women did the cooking and the cleaning. Of course, if Skip had offered to fix dinner once in a while, I wouldn't have turned him down."

She looked at Cam to judge his reaction. Apparently their relationship had progressed to the point where she could mention her late husband without the two of them automatically getting uptight.

"How about some dinner music?" Cam asked as he slid open a panel in the side of the table.

"Sure."

Jo expected Chopin or Mozart. Instead when the eight-speaker system sprang to life, it delivered a Kenny Rogers ballad about two teenagers whose love finally triumphed over the long arm of the law.

"I like Kenny Rogers."

"I thought you might."

"If you'd rather hear something else—"

"I've got eclectic musical tastes." Pressing some buttons, he adjusted the speakers. "The system can reproduce any size effects from a large concert hall to a small cabaret. What's your choice?"

She closed her eyes for a minute. "Let's pretend we've got lawn seating at Oregon Ridge."

He laughed. "You're a cheap date." When he held out his arms, she nestled against him as they listened to the rest of the song.

The smile curving her lips froze as the phone rang.

Jo's eyes riveted to the brass telephone on the end table. Cam followed her gaze. "It's all right. He's not going to call you here."

She nodded tightly.

Cam picked up the receiver. It was a business discussion, and her host was obviously uncomfortable talking in front of Jo.

"I'll clean up while you're busy," she mouthed.

He nodded. "Sorry."

Jo loaded the tray. In the kitchen, she put the trash in the compactor, rinsed the dishes and stacked them in the dishwasher. Cam didn't appear. To give him some more time, she made coffee. When she brought it in, he was just putting down the phone. There was a scowl on his face.

She set the coffee cups down. "Problems?"

"Nothing that can't be straightened out. I've got Phil Mercer working on it."

Instinct told her he was being evasive. "You didn't get to work at all today, did you?"

"No." He reached up and pulled her down beside him onto the thick rug.

"Is there anything I can do to help?"

"Yes."

His mouth slanted over hers with a kiss that should have driven every coherent thought out of her mind. When he lifted his head, she gave it one more try. "Don't get your priorities screwed up because of me."

"Honey, I'm not. I don't think I've ever had my priorities in better order."

He lowered her to her back, trapping her body between his hard length and the plush rug. The feelings that had been simmering between them during dinner came to a full, rolling boil.

She could come to no harm when she was in his arms. The knowledge was as liberating as it was arousing.

With primitive urgency they began to explore each other's bodies, twisting and arching together with the need to get closer and closer still. If there was a note of desperation in Cam's lovemaking, Jo didn't question its source.

SOMETIME during the evening they moved upstairs to Cam's bedroom. When Jo woke up at seven in the morning, she was naked with the covers down around her waist, and Cam was lying on his side, his gray gaze locked on her.

She reached down to drag up the sheet, but he pulled her back into a tight embrace.

"I thought guys slowed down after thirty."

"You do potent things to my hormones. Or maybe it's because I'm falling in love with you."

Her eyes flew open. "Are you teasing me?"

"I wouldn't tease you about something like that."

"Oh, Cam—I—don't know what to say."

"I'll let you get used to the idea."

He began to kiss her and touch her once more. Now there was a tenderness in his lovemaking that made her heart ache to be able to return his declaration. But it was too soon. She had to know that she wasn't just turning to him in a crisis. She had to know her feelings would stand the test of time, because if she ever got married again, it was going to be for keeps.

He seemed to sense her mood as she got dressed later and followed him downstairs. As they made breakfast, she saw his pragmatic, empirical persona slip back into place.

"I have to put in an appearance at Randolph Enterprises," he told her.

"You can't spend all your time chaperoning me."

"There's another car in the garage. A BMW. Why don't you drive that down to Light Street, and I'll meet you for lunch."

"If you can't get away, I'll understand."

"I'll get away."

"Do you mind if I make a few phone calls here? It's early enough so I might be able to catch some of the women who weren't home yesterday."

"Of course not."

Before Cam left, he gave her the keys to the car and the house and showed her how to set the security system—which was much more elaborate than hers. Then he gave her a bear hug. "Take care of yourself."

"I will," she promised.

Jo decided to use the phone in the den. As she sat down at Cam's desk, she was amused to note that all his mail was sorted into labeled cubbyholes. At least if she married him, he'd organize the clutter that swirled around her. Or would the disorganization drive him bananas?

She smiled, suddenly optimistic that they'd somehow work things out.

Just as she was reaching for the phone, it rang. Jo tensed. Until this was over, she was going to be suspicious of all incoming calls, she acknowledged. But it could be Cam with something he'd forgotten to tell her.

"Hello?"

"Angel face! Did you think you could hide from me?"

Her heart started to pound and she almost slammed the receiver back into the cradle. Then she realized Laughing Boy was handing her an opportunity. This was the first time she'd talked to him since she'd interviewed some of his other victims. "How did you get this number?" she asked, hoping her voice sounded calm.

"I have my ways."

"I've talked to some of the other women you've bothered."

He laughed. "So?"

"What have you got against redheads?"

"Wouldn't you like to know?"

His mood was different, Jo noted. He wasn't bombarding her with sexual innuendos. This time, even through the electronic filter, she detected a note of tension. Good. Maybe he was worried because she'd gotten somewhere with the phone company.

"I know something you don't," he taunted.

"What?"

"Something about Randolph."

Despite her resolve not to let him get to her, she clutched the receiver. "Cam?"

"There are some very interesting things your boyfriend would rather you not know."

"Are you going to tell me what they are?"

"No. I think it would be more fun for you to find out by yourself, miss hotshot detective. But I'll give you a hint to get you started. Go back to those old files of your husband's. The ones involving cases he didn't talk to you about."

"Which case?"

"Oh, I'm sure you'll figure it out." Before Jo could ask another question, the line went dead, and she was left with white knuckles clutched around the receiver. What possible connection could there be between Cam and one of Skip's cases?

Nothing! she told herself firmly. The jerk was just trying to rattle her. But now she had to crush the seed of doubt he'd planted—before it took root and started poisoning her mind. Instead of making phone calls to the other women on the list, she'd better go right to the office and check back through the files.

On her way to the garage, however, Jo hesitated for a moment. Laughing Boy had called and maneuvered her into checking her files. Was he outside somewhere waiting for her to leave Cam's house? Maybe this was just a ploy to get her out in the open where he could pounce. Cautiously she looked out both the downstairs and up-stairs windows. As far as she could see, no one was lurk-ing around. If he were around the corner, Cam's BMW could certainly outrun just about anything he had.

Her prediction about the car proved correct. It was fast and powerful and a joy to drive. After whipping around several blocks, Jo was sure no one was following her. But as she approached the garage on Light Street, she began to tense up again. Her tormentor knew where she was going. He didn't have to follow her to the office to scoop her up.

Jo circled the block, once more looking for suspicious cars or pedestrians. On a downtown street, it was diffi-cult to determine whether the panhandler on the corner was collecting money for his next bottle of Wild Turkey or watching for her.

She hesitated at the entrance to the garage where she usually parked. Then instead of driving inside, she pulled up in the loading zone in back of 43 Light Street. From there it was only a few steps inside the building. In the basement she found Lou and asked if he'd mind parking the car. He was quick to oblige.

"I wish they'd catch the guy who's botherin' you," he muttered.

"They will," Jo assured him. As she took the elevator up, she sagged back against the wall and closed her eyes. Over the years she'd worked for a number of women who were being harassed or threatened. She'd been sympa-thetic, but she'd never really understood the sense of de-fenselessness—the growing terror as you lost control of your life. Now she did.

As she walked down the hall to the office, a man stepped out of the shadows. Jo stopped short, her heart in her throat. She'd been so careful, and he was already in the building waiting for her! She was about to turn and dash for the stairs when he called her name.

"Ms. O'Malley. Wait. It's Detective Hamill."

"I'm sorry, I thought—"

"I didn't mean to startle you."

"I guess I'm just jumpy this morning."

"I called you, but you must have left Randolph's house. So I took a chance on intercepting you here."

The grim set of his mouth and the tone of his voice put her on guard. "Something's happened."

"Yes. Can we go inside your office?"

As Jo unlocked the door and flipped on the lights, she felt her stomach clench. Turning to face him, she steeled herself for something unpleasant.

"We found Eddie Cahill's ex-wife early this morning. There's no way to put a good face on this, so I'll just give it to you straight. She was beaten and murdered."

Chapter Eleven

With all the focus on redheads and weddings, Jo hadn't been thinking much about Eddie Cahill's wife. News of her death was the last thing Jo had been prepared to hear.

A gasp escaped her lips. "Oh, poor Karen." Suddenly she knew her legs wouldn't support her. Before she could embarrass herself by falling on her face, she dropped into one of the visitor's chairs opposite the desk. Hamill brought her a drink of water from the cooler, and she sipped gratefully.

"I know it's a shock."

"I suppose Eddie did it."

"There's no hard evidence yet."

"What about Jennifer Stark? Is she okay?"

"The prosecuting attorney? I understand she's taken an extended leave of absence."

"Yeah." Jo sat numbly clutching her paper cup while the officer told her what they knew about the murder. Karen had been reported missing by her mother the night before. Under the circumstances, the department had mounted an extensive search. Her partially clothed body had been found near Loch Raven reservoir by a man walking his doberman that morning. "The dog pulled the guy off the path and into the underbrush," Hamill said.

"There wasn't much attempt to hide the body. It was almost as if the murderer wanted it to be found."

"Where does that leave me?" Jo asked.

"We can keep a tail on you for a few days, and we'll certainly increase the patrols near your home and office and Mr. Randolph's town house. I'd also like to suggest putting a decoy in your house—a policewoman with your general physical characteristics."

That wasn't Jo's usual style, but she agreed.

"You didn't think Cahill was going to make good on his threats, did you?" she asked.

Hamill looked embarrassed. "You know what kind of constraints we operate under. When he wasn't recaptured immediately, there was no way we could put you or his ex-wife under indefinite surveillance."

Jo nodded. That was what she'd told Cam.

"Do you have an extra key to your house?" Hamill asked.

Jo produced one from her desk drawer. "I'll get a few more things I need this afternoon. Then the place is all yours."

Hamill's visit left Jo feeling strangely lethargic—as if she hadn't slept in days and couldn't summon the energy to cross the room. Partly, she acknowledged, it was guilt. Last year she was the one who'd told Karen Cahill that she was going to have to go to the D.A. with the information about her husband's drug dealing. Now he'd killed her.

On the other hand, it was Karen who had come to her with the request for some ammunition she could use in a divorce case. At the moment, the circular reasoning was too much for Jo. Finally she forced herself to get out of the chair and go over to the large storage closet where she'd stuffed Skip's out-of-date records.

They were stacked in cardboard boxes, and the thought of shuffling through all of them made her even more weary. But she forced herself to start the task.

It was too much trouble to carry the boxes to her desk. Instead she heaped them in a semicircle on the floor, sat down in the middle, and began to dig through them.

It didn't take long before she began to get interested in the project—particularly after she came across the first case she and Skip had worked on together. They'd both posed as street people and staked out Fells Point to catch the runaway daughter of an old Baltimore family.

There were other cases, many of which she'd worked on. Finally she came across a box that contained folders Skip had kept to himself. Some of the assignments had been before she'd come to work for him. Despite her protests, others had been jobs he'd considered too dangerous to involve his wife. And a few had been situations where clients had insisted on strict confidentiality.

As Jo thumbed through the last two categories, her eyes bounced off one of the names, and she stopped dead. Where her fingers touched the manila folder, they seemed to burn. The tab read Randolph Enterprises. Cam certainly hadn't mentioned anything about that.

With a feeling of dread, she pulled the file from the box and began to read Skip's carefully penned notes.

Morgan Randolph, Cam's father, had hired Skip to find out who was responsible for a series of disturbing incidents. Randolph products still in development were showing up in the commercial lines of competitors. That must be the industrial espionage episode Cam had told her about, Jo thought, with a little sigh of relief. He hadn't tried to hide that from her when she'd asked.

Yet he hadn't said a word about Skip being on the case. Hadn't he known?

She got her answer several pages down, when she found a carbon of a letter from Skip to Cam requesting a list of compromised projects. His detailed reply was clipped to the carbon. Jo leaned back against the wall.

So Cam *had* dealt with Skip. But most of her husband's contacts had probably been with the father. Perhaps Cam hadn't remembered the detective's name.

With shaky fingers, she turned more pages. There was also a memo from Cam's older brother Collin Randolph. Since he was in charge of personnel, he had listed employees he thought Skip ought to check. From Skip's subsequent reports, it appeared that none of those investigations had panned out.

Reading between the lines, Jo gathered that the elder Randolph had started pressing for results. Skip's next tack had been a background check on the members of the Randolph family. Jo breathed a sigh of relief when she saw that there was nothing questionable in Cam's background. About his only indiscretion had been to get drunk at a couple of parties in his freshman year at Dartmouth.

The next report was on Collin. He'd also been a model college student. Interestingly, he'd had hardly any social life when he'd lived in the dorm at Brown. Former classmates had spoken of him as not being particularly friendly. Things had changed when he'd come back to Baltimore to work in the family company. Sporadically at first and then on a regular basis, he'd begun frequenting gay bars. Jo paused as she digested that bit of information. According to Skip, Collin had hidden his homosexuality from his family, even when he'd developed relationships with several men who became more than casual lovers.

Skip had handled the revelations discreetly. He'd quietly gone to the older Randolph brother with the information and asked if there was anybody who might be taking advantage of him because they knew about his secret life. Collin had responded in a very flat, emotionless manner and had assured Skip that his private life would not put the company in jeopardy. Two days later, he had stuck a pistol in his mouth and pulled the trigger.

Jo's hands clenched the edge of the paper. How tragic. No wonder Cam hadn't wanted to talk about the case. It had inadvertently led to his brother's death.

She almost put the file away. But there were a few sheets of paper left. Under an obituary in the *Baltimore Sun* was an official letter from Morgan dismissing Skip from the case along with payment of $2,000 to cover his expenses to date.

The final entry in the file was the summary of a conversation Skip had had with Cameron Randolph a month later. Morgan Randolph had just died of a heart attack. An angry Cam had called to accuse Skip of destroying the family. According to Cam, Skip hadn't been asked to investigate family members. Furthermore, the dirt he'd dug up had driven Collin to suicide, and their father had never recovered from the shock of his son's death. Which meant that he was responsible for not just one but two deaths. Skip's notes added that Cam had threatened to put him out of business.

Jo closed the file and let her head flop back against the wall, fighting the sick feeling that had begun to churn in her stomach. Cam had never mentioned that he'd known Skip. But they'd certainly been acquainted. More to the point, he'd worked himself up into an irrational hatred for her husband. Now she thought back over all the subtle and not so subtle signals Cam had given off when

Skip's name had entered the conversation. She'd assumed Cam was just jealous because she'd been married before. Viewed in this new light, Cam's behavior suggested open hostility to Skip. Just where did that leave her?

With fingers that felt as if they'd been numbed in an ice storm, she shuffled through the papers again, scanning disjointed paragraphs and sentences, somehow hoping that things would look different on a second reading. As she was skimming the paragraph on Collin's college career, a knock at the door made her jump. Her head jerked up. Through the glass she recognized a familiar silhouette.

When she got up and unlocked the door, there was a smile on Cam's lips. It quickly faded when he saw the grim expression on her face.

"What happened?"

She considered the question for several heartbeats. "Well, for starters, it looks like Eddie Cahill made good his threats against Karen. She was beaten and murdered."

"Oh, Jo— Honey, I'm sorry." He moved to fold her into his arms but she evaded his embrace. "What else is wrong?"

"I have the feeling you can figure it out if you really try."

He looked from her to the stacks of boxes and open folder on the floor. "You were going back through Skip's old files." On the surface his voice was flat but Jo could hear the edge of tension he was trying to control.

"And I've been reading his notes on the industrial espionage at Randolph Enterprises. Why didn't you tell me the whole story when we had our frank little discussion about the EMP?"

"It wasn't relevant."

"Not relevant! Sheez!" Jo stamped her foot, paced to the window and then whirled back toward him. "What wasn't relevant? That you blamed my husband for your brother's death—and your father's? Or that you were just getting close to me so you could figure out a way to put me out of business—the way you threatened to do with Skip?"

He winced as he faced her across the room. "I'd decided you didn't have anything to do with that."

"From your investigations of me, you mean?"

"Yes. And personal observation."

"How magnanimous of you."

"Okay, I admit it. Meeting you brought it all back." He swallowed convulsively. "All the sorrow and all the anger. Right after I realized who you were, I decided to see what I could find out about you—with some vague idea of settling the score."

She muttered something unladylike under her breath and folded her arms across her chest.

"Jo, I swear," he continued, "as I started getting to know you, I felt horrible about our relationship not being honest. Then when I realized that you were more important to me than anything that had happened in the past, I just wanted to keep from destroying what was developing between us."

"Did you think I wasn't going to find out about your letter to Skip?"

"I was going to tell you—later."

"Sheez!"

"I'm not very good at this sort of thing."

"You're right about that."

"Jo, please—"

She shook her head before he could finish the sentence. "It's pretty hard for me to operate on an open, honest level with someone who isn't being open and honest with me." Her eyes drilled into him.

The accusing look on her face would have made a lesser man drop his gaze. Cam held his ground. After several silent moments, it was Jo who felt too uncomfortable to continue the standoff. She looked away.

"Dishonesty isn't my strong suit," Cam said. "I knew I'd made a mistake. I was trying to work my way out of it—without losing you."

"Do you still think Skip was responsible for your brother's death? And your father's?"

"Jo, I—"

"Do you?"

"He wasn't authorized to go digging into our family."

"What do you mean he wasn't authorized? Your father hired him to find out who was stealing Randolph product designs, and he was conducting the investigation according to his best judgment. He was authorized to do anything he needed to do to get the job done. He hadn't turned up anything on the employees. The next logical step was to see if someone in the family was responsible."

"He should have cleared that with my father."

"What if your father was the one involved?"

"My father hired him, for God sakes."

"Weirder things have happened in this business. People torching their own warehouses to get the insurance money. Clients hiring a private investigator and laying a trail of clues leading to someone else."

"My father wouldn't have done that."

"Then let's go back to the facts and try to figure out what did happen. I gather from our previous conversation that the espionage stopped after your brother's death. That suggests that it did have something to do with him. Maybe one of his gay friends had threatened to go to your father if Collin didn't cooperate. Collin knew the revelation would crush your father, so he complied.''

''That's preposterous. I won't have you besmirching my brother's memory.''

''I'm drawing logical conclusions from the information in that file. You ought to understand that. You're big on logic, aren't you?''

He glared at her.

''Your father didn't let Skip continue the investigation after Collin died. Perhaps if he had, we wouldn't be standing here making guesses about what caused the information leak at Randolph Enterprises.''

''You're a lot like Skip, aren't you?''

''If you mean logical, dependable, persistent, fair-minded, yes.''

''Fair-minded!''

''A private investigator has to put personal biases aside when he takes on a case.''

''And he or she doesn't care about who gets hurt as a result of the investigation,'' Cam grated.

''Of course we do. But facts are facts.''

''Facts are facts,'' he repeated sarcastically.

''And while we're on that subject, what was it that you were trying to hide from me last night when Phil Mercer called? Or were you even talking to Mr. Mercer?''

''Certainly I was talking to Mercer. He was following up on an assignment I gave him. I was trying to find out how someone could have gotten into your house to screw around with your television set when your Randolph Enterprises security system was on.''

''And?''

"I'm still working on it," he clipped out.

"Why didn't you want to tell me about it?"

"I was upset about the system failure and wanted to wait until I had some answers."

"But you didn't trust me enough to get my input."

"Trust wasn't the issue."

"Don't you think I have a right to be angry with you? And I'm not talking about the damn security system. It's the business with Skip."

"Yes. You have the right to be angry," he admitted in a low voice.

"At least we've reached a point of agreement."

Cam sighed. "Jo, I think we're both too upset to be having a rational discussion." He waited for some sign that might contradict the statement. When it wasn't forthcoming, he walked slowly toward the door.

Anger and Jo's need to defend Skip had kept her going during the argument. Now her throat was too raw with unshed tears to call him back. As he carefully closed the door, they welled up in her eyes. But the emotional release gave her no comfort. Deep inside she ached from a mixture of outrage, hurt and sadness.

THE MAN panhandling on the street corner across from 43 Light Street glanced up with interest as Cameron Randolph stalked out of the building. The defeated look on the inventor's face brought him an immense surge of pleasure. Jo had checked her late husband's files and discovered that mister rich-and-powerful Randolph wasn't such a nice guy after all.

He turned his head toward the rough brick wall and hunched his shoulder as if he were shielding his body from the wind. He was really hiding the smirk that had plastered itself across his features. He'd won a major victory this afternoon. He'd pried Jo O'Malley away from that smart bastard. It was only a matter of time before he got the rest of what he wanted.

He spotted a plainclothes policeman also dressed like a panhandler working the other end of the block across from Ms. O'Malley's building. The irony didn't escape him and he couldn't hold back a little giggle.

He wasn't stupid enough to try to scoop Denise up now when the heat was on.

He blinked and felt a momentary wave of confusion. Denise. No, this one was named Jo O'Malley. Or was she Denise? She looked like angelic little Denise. But she wasn't going to get the chance to hurt him the way Denise had. This time he was the one who was going to call the shots.

He wanted her to know how much power he had over her. Then he'd show her his brass bed in the wedding chapel.

OVER THE NEXT FEW WEEKS, Jo's life evolved into a strange motif. She felt as if she were simply going through the motions of living—without any rhyme or reason to her existence. Her further attempts to find out who had made the phone calls to the other women turned up nothing. Since she was barely capable of functioning, she wasn't surprised.

If the period before Abby's wedding was marked by anything for her, it was chiefly the lack of any regular routine. Jo varied the time at which she left for the office and when she came home. She wore a changing array of disguises that would have done central casting proud. She used the back entrance to 43 Light Street as often as the front. She rented a series of cars—never driving one for more than a couple of days. Some afternoons she gathered up a handful of the files she'd need and tried to work from one of her temporary homes. Devising and carrying out the precautions became a game on which she could focus. It was better than dwelling on the disappointment of discovering that the future she'd dared to imagine with Cameron Randolph was just a stupid fantasy.

As soon as Laura heard about what had happened, she quickly invited Jo to stay with her. Jo gratefully accepted—on condition that she minimize any danger to her friend by making arrangements at the last minute and never over the phone. She also found she could count on a warm support group ready to help her in any way they could. Noel Emery, Laura's secretary, and Abby's mother also volunteered to put her up. So Jo bounced between the extremes of a lumpy sofa bed in Noel's tiny living room and a plush suite in the Franklin mansion.

There were still wedding activities at which her presence would have been expected. But everybody understood that Jo could be in danger, which turned out to be the perfect excuse for ducking out. She skipped the mixed groups where Cam would be on the scene and only attended a couple of the showers and luncheons that were just for the female contingent. And she avoided getting into any serious discussions with Abby.

But the Wednesday before the wedding, Abby showed up at Jo's office with a bag from the deli.

"I brought us some lunch," she announced. "A hamburger and French fries for you and chicken salad with sprouts for me."

"Thanks."

"I need the company. Every time I'm alone, I start getting the jitters," the bride-to-be admitted.

"You?"

Abby unwrapped a straw and twirled it between her fingers. "No matter how much you think you love someone, getting married is a big step."

"Yeah."

"I missed you at the Stacys' reception last night."

Jo slowly chewed a bite of hamburger. "You know why I wasn't there."

"For two reasons. One of them is certainly valid. But you can't keep avoiding Cam."

"Sure I can."

"What about the rehearsal dinner Friday?"

"I can skip the dinner and just come to the walk-through."

"Jo, please."

The detective wadded her hamburger wrapper into a ball and pitched it at the trash can. It bounced off the edge and landed on the floor. "I don't think you have the jitters. I think you came up here with lunch so we could talk about how stupid I've been acting."

"Do you think you've been acting stupid?"

"No, Dr. Franklin. I think I'm being perfectly realistic about my nonrelationship with Cameron Randolph. It's over."

The psychologist sighed. "It's kind of a conflict of interest counseling both you and Cam. That's why I haven't brought up the heated conversation that ended with you ordering him out of your office."

"Is that what he told you? Well, I didn't order him out of the office. He was the one who said he was going to leave."

"Just seeing if I could get a rise out of you. Your emotions have been as flat as a loaf of pita bread lately."

Jo sat up straighter in her chair. "Just what the hell did Cameron Randolph say to you?"

"Do I detect a tiny spark of interest in your question?"

"No. All right, yes."

"If Cam were a patient, I'd have to consider the things he told me confidential."

"He's a friend."

"A good friend," Abby agreed. "He's also a man whose mother died when he was a little boy. His father and his older brother raised him. How do you think it made him feel when one of them committed suicide and the other had a fatal heart attack within a matter of weeks?"

Jo dragged a cold French fry through the catsup and laid it back on the paper plate. "Bad," she murmured without raising her head.

"Devastated is more like it. The loss of his brother and his father one right after the other was the worst thing that ever happened to him—and that was coupled with the shock of finding out that the brother he loved had been hiding a secret life from his family."

Jo's whole body was charged with tension, but the only sign was in the bloodless caps of her knuckles where she'd clenched her fingers.

"He had to find a way to deal with it," Abby continued. "Unfortunately part of his coping mechanism was looking for someone to blame."

"Too bad it was Skip. And me." Jo didn't allow her voice to reflect her churning emotions.

"Over the past few weeks he's had time to think about his own motivations—and about how his behavior affected your relationship."

"He hasn't called to share his insights with me."

"He's terrified to face you."

Jo laughed mirthlessly.

In contrast, her friend continued in a calm voice. "One thing about a man like Cam, when he chooses a course of action, it's hard to see things any differently. As he got to know you, the relationship cast a whole bunch of earlier assumptions he'd made in doubt. He had a terrible time dealing with that."

"If he'd come clean with me up-front, it would have been a lot better."

"Would it? Can you honestly picture him calling you up the morning after my parents' party and telling you he blamed Skip for the major tragedy in his life?"

Put that way, the suggestion was ludicrous, Jo admitted.

"Even if he'd waited until he knew you a little better, with your hot temper and your sense of loyalty to Skip, you would have given him the heave-ho."

Jo nodded slowly. "You're probably right. But there had to be some better way than what he did."

"Hindsight is wonderful, isn't it?"

Jo flushed.

"There's no point in speculating on what might have happened," Abby continued. "Now that you've both had a chance to cool down, why don't you talk about it? A lot of major misunderstandings between people could be cleared up if they'd just sit down and have a sensible conversation."

"I said some things he didn't want to hear."

"He said things you didn't want to hear."

"Yeah. Like about Skip."

"Perhaps you made him realize that his feelings toward Skip were a defense mechanism," Abby said gently.

"I did?"

"The only way you'll find out for sure is to talk to him about it," Abby reiterated.

Jo was silent for a moment. Finally, she took a deep breath. "You think he—uh—that he still—?"

"Yes." Abby's voice was full of encouragement.

"He hurt me—with the stuff he said about Skip."

"But how does he make you feel otherwise?"

"What if it was all wishful thinking on my part?"

"Do you really believe that?"

"Abby, I know it doesn't make perfect sense, but in a way, after Skip died, I felt like he'd let me down. I mean, I'd opened up and let myself lean on him. Then he pulled the rug out from under me." She looked pleadingly at her friend.

"A lot of people feel that way when a loved one dies."

Jo sighed. "I felt guilty about that for a long time. And then, you know, I was just getting to the point where I thought I could take a chance on Cam . . ."

"Sometimes you have to take a chance to get what you want."

The two women ate in silence for several minutes, neither one of them making much progress with the meal. Finally Abby wrapped up her half-eaten sandwich and stood up. "I'd better get back to my office. I've got a patient coming at one o'clock."

"Thanks for lunch. And for . . . provoking me."

Abby grinned. "No charge."

After her friend left, Jo sat staring out the window at the office building across the alley. For the first time in weeks, she felt the dark cloud that had been hovering over her begin to lift. She had only thought about certain parts of that last angry conversation with Cam. Now she allowed herself to remember the look on his face and some of the things he'd said. He'd talked about sorrow and anger, but she hadn't let herself react to the pain in his voice. When he'd said he'd been afraid of losing her, she'd been thinking that he already had.

Now she couldn't help wondering what it would be like to see him again. The more she wondered, the more she felt something tender and protective inside her chest swell with hope.

Abby had said you had to take risks to get what you wanted. Wasn't everything in life a risk?

What was the worst thing that could happen, she asked herself. That she and Cam couldn't work things out. Well, Abby had made her see one thing pretty clearly: they didn't have a chance the way things stood.

The wedding rehearsal would be neutral territory. Maybe if he didn't make the first move, she would.

THE NEXT EVENING as she stood before the ornately carved cheval glass in Laura's guest room, Jo surveyed her appearance with more interest than she'd shown in weeks. The strain of hiding and of being estranged from Cam had both taken their toll. She'd lost weight, and her face was pale. She'd compensated with a bit more makeup than she usually used. Earlier that afternoon she'd driven her rental car out to Columbia and found a silk shift at Woodies that helped camouflage her thin figure.

Dinner was in a private room upstairs at the Brass Elephant, an elegant restaurant in a restored town house on Charles Street. Its unusual name came from the brass fixtures throughout the building that were shaped like elephant heads. Steve had been pleased with the choice of location because he knew Abby was providing a little reminder of his years in India. The meal would be followed by a walk-through at the Greenspring Valley Church where Abby and Steve were getting married.

To minimize the risks to Jo, Abby had waited until the last minute to make firm arrangements for the party. It was understood that Jo and Laura would arrive a bit after the stated dinner hour and slip in a back door of the restaurant. Jo wasn't thinking about security as she and Laura drove down to Charles Street. In fact, she could hardly contain the keen feeling of anticipation that had been building ever since she'd talked to Abby that afternoon.

Her steps were quick as she hurried toward the little dining room several steps ahead of Laura. When she walked through the archway, she noticed two things almost simultaneously. The bride-to-be was looking anxiously toward the door. And Cameron Randolph was conspicuously absent from among the assembled members of the wedding party.

Chapter Twelve

The minute Abby spotted the maid of honor, she came rushing forward. "Oh, Jo, I'm so sorry. He called a few minutes ago to say he wouldn't be here." There was no need to name the man they were talking about.

Jo tried to keep the disappointment off her face.

Abby squeezed her hand. "I don't know what to say. I shouldn't have gotten your hopes up."

"It's not your fault." Jo turned quickly away toward the bar that had been set up in the corner. She didn't really want anything to drink. Still, she needed a few minutes to pull herself together before she faced the happy throng assembled to honor Steve and Abby.

Cam didn't show up for the actual rehearsal, either. Jo found herself playing her matron of honor role opposite an empty spot on the stone floor.

It was no less empty than the hollow that had opened up inside her chest. She'd gotten her hopes up, and they'd been dashed.

She went through the rehearsal in a daze, unaware that her friends had thrown a sort of protective net around her—both physically and emotionally.

But the man standing in the shadows at the back of the church with neck rigid and jaw clenched was very aware of what was happening.

Denise...

Jo O'Malley...

Denise...

They were together in church again.

The first time he'd seen her standing under the stained-glass windows, it was like a light from heaven had streamed in on both of them.

Watching her now, the feeling came back, strong and sure the way it had been in the beginning. He needed her again.

The craving to have her with him once more almost choked him, almost choked off all rational thought. Sudden energy surged through his body, and he almost started up the aisle. Then at the last minute, he caught himself. Not now when everybody was watching. But soon. He had the power. And when he chose to use it, no one could stand in his way.

IT WAS STRANGE, Jo thought as she stood in front of the inexpensive door mirror in Noel's hallway, how different she felt this morning. The dime-store looking glass reflected back a slightly distorted image, elongating the middle of her body as if to accent her recently acquired gauntness.

She tugged at her skirt. But that didn't make it hang any better over her bony hips. Two months ago when Abby had selected the elaborate blue velvet gown, Jo had simply felt overdressed in the rich creation. Now she was going to feel like an out-and-out fool walking down the aisle.

Except that no one was going to be looking at her, she told herself. They'd all be focused on Steve and Abby. Maybe she could even slip away right after the receiving line and come back here to lick her wounds.

She hadn't slept much. She hadn't been able to choke down more than a cup of weak tea for breakfast. And she hadn't been able to get her mind off Cameron Randolph.

After that talk with Abby, she'd been stupid enough to be optimistic. Well, Abby had made a mistake in her analysis of Cam. Because she was in love and getting married, she'd blithely assumed that the rest of the couples in the world would work out their problems.

She made an effort to bring her mind back to the wedding. At least there was one thing to look forward to. Whoever was making calls to redheaded maids of honor almost always stopped as soon as the big event was over. After today, she'd only have to worry about Eddie Cahill, she thought with a grim little laugh.

All her cynicism evaporated, however, when she walked into the room at the back of the church where Abby and her attendants were waiting for the service to begin.

The bride looked radiant and excited and nervous in her taffeta gown studded with tiny pearls. When she smiled uncertainly at her, Jo crossed the room and embraced her friend.

"I'm so sorry about last night," Abby apologized again.

"It's all right. Really. Don't let anything spoil today." Jo took a step back. "You look beautiful."

"Thank you. So do you."

Jo stifled the automatic denial that sprang to her lips. If the bride wanted to entertain that kind of fantasy, why put up a protest?

Laura and two friends who'd gone to school with Abby fluttered around trying to make conversation. They were all a bit teary as they listened to the organ music drifting in from the chapel.

Finally one of the deacons and Abby's father appeared at the door and told them it was show time. He didn't look any too calm himself, Jo thought as his daughter took his arm and they started for the back of the church. Probably they were both glad they didn't have to walk down the aisle alone.

Which was not the case with Jo. The bouquet of rosebuds and baby's breath trembled in her hands as she followed them out. She glanced at the private security guard stationed by the door. He was there for her, she thought and squeezed her eyes shut for a minute. *Don't let anything mess up Abby's wedding,* she prayed silently as she took her place at the central portal.

In front of her, the church was filled to capacity, the crowd waiting in hushed expectation.

Then, as the organ music reached a crescendo, Jo was marching down the aisle, her eyes fixed on the stained-glass window above the altar so that she saw the assemblage on either side of her only in her peripheral vision. The bridesmaids and ushers had already taken their places amid the red roses perfuming the chancel. Then the organist began to play Wagner's traditional wedding march. A minute later, Abby and her father joined the group in front of the altar.

The music stopped, and a door to the right of the choir opened. The groom and his best man stepped out. Jo knew she had been waiting for this moment. She was sure all other eyes were focused on Steve, but she couldn't take hers off Cam. Her breath caught in her throat as once more she was struck by how incredibly handsome he looked in a tuxedo. Except that now his face was pale and his features were drawn. Only his eyes held the energy she remembered. They seemed to glitter in the warm light of the chapel as they locked with hers. For a dizzying moment, some wordless communication passed between them.

"This is the day the Lord has made. Let us rejoice and be glad in it," the minister said.

Cam continued to watch her intently. She gave him an uncertain smile, and he nodded almost imperceptibly.

"God created us male and female, and gave us marriage so that husband and wife may help and comfort each other, living faithfully together in plenty and in want, in joy and sorrow..."

The words took on a special meaning as she and Cam stared at each other. In front of her, she heard Steve and Abby exchanging vows.

"Abby, do you take Steve to be your husband and promise before God and these witnesses to be his loving and faithful wife...?"

"I do."

Jo saw Cam's expression soften. Her hand reached out toward him. When she realized they were standing five feet apart, she dropped her arm back to her side. A current seemed to flow between them. Or was it just because she wanted to believe in the power of love?

When the service was over, the organ music swelled up as Steve and Abby kissed. At the same time, Jo felt emotion swell in her chest.

With radiant smiles on their faces, the newly married couple hurried back down the aisle. Cam's eyes were not on the bride and groom. He was staring at Jo. He caught her hand and simply held it for a moment as if he'd forgotten where they were. Then they fell into place behind Steve and Abby. As they reached the back of the church, the rest of the party automatically headed for the limousines waiting to take them to the reception. Cam looked around, and Jo had the feeling he was about to pull her out of the line. Then one of the deacons appeared and ushered them out to the waiting cars. They piled in beside Laura and another bridesmaid.

"We have to talk," Cam whispered.

"Yes."

But there was no opportunity for a private conversation as the car sped toward the exclusive Greenspring Valley country club where the reception was being held. And there was no chance to talk as they stood in the endless receiving line making polite conversation with friends and family.

Jo felt a thousand butterflies clamoring for attention in her stomach. Beside her, she could feel Cam's tension building. Her own nerves were drawing as tight as an overwound clock spring. She shifted from one foot to the other as she gave Cam little sideways glances.

Finally he muttered something under his breath, grabbed her hand, and yanked her out of the line. "I think they can finish without us," he commented as he looked around for a place where they could be alone. The lobby was crowded with elegantly dressed guests, and heads turned in their direction as they made their way through the throng.

Cam didn't waver. His face set in determined lines, he pulled Jo through double doors and they found themselves in the serving pantry off the kitchen, surrounded by rolling carts of food destined for the buffet tables.

"I thought you knew where you were going," Jo observed.

Cam shrugged. "I'm through hiding from you. We have to talk. Now."

As they stood facing each other, words seemed to freeze in Jo's throat. And Cam wasn't doing much better.

Suddenly the ice jam broke and apologies came tumbling out.

"I didn't mean to hurt you."

"I should have called you."

"I don't know what I was thinking about."

"I—"

Before the sentence could be completed, the door flew open, and a man bolted into the room.

Startled, they both whirled to face him. Suddenly details registered in Jo's mind: the brown hair. The scar on the right side of his upper lip. The malevolent look in those dark eyes she remembered from that day in court.

Eddie Cahill.

From under his coat, he pulled a sawed-off shotgun.

"You thought you were so clever switching cars and houses. But I've been watching you and I've got you now, Ms. Super Detective," he gloated, his voice seething with hate. "When you play hardball with Eddie Cahill, you'd better watch your back."

Time seemed to slow as Jo shrank away from the man who had been stalking her for weeks. He had killed Karen. He had said he was going to kill her, too. He was going to do it. Now. Just when she and Cam had found each other again. In his face, she saw how much he was enjoying her agony and his triumph.

Out of the corner of her eye, she detected a slight movement. Cam was edging toward Eddie.

No! The warning was frozen in her throat.

The gun wavered as if Eddie had suddenly become aware that he and Jo weren't the only people in the room. At that moment, her hip bumped against one of the serving carts. Another, heaped with shrimp and cocktail sauce, was immediately to her left. Acting on desperate reflex, she reached out and shoved it with all her might toward the man who had sworn to kill her. It plowed into his waist, and Eddie grunted just as the gun went off. The shot went wild. Plump shrimp and red cocktail sauce flew into the air—some of it landing on Jo's dress and the rest splattering to the floor.

Cam dived toward Eddie and wrestled him to the tile. There was another shot as they fought for the gun.

"Cam, Cam," Jo screamed, her voice at last unfrozen.

The shots had attracted attention, and moments later, the door flew open. Steve Claiborne bounded into the room, his face grim, his body primed for action. Behind him, moving more slowly, was one of the Franklins' security guards. He was staggering and holding his chin.

Jo barely noticed the intrusion. Her eyes were glued to the men at her feet. One of them had been shot. But who?

They stopped struggling, and a groan issued from the tangled pile of arms and legs. Jo's whole body went rigid with tension. For several seconds, nothing happened. Then Cam slowly sat up. He was holding the gun. And Eddie Cahill was holding his side. Blood oozed from between his clenched fingers.

As Steve swiftly assessed the damage, Jo dropped down beside Cam. "Are you all right?"

"Yes."

"Thank God." She was reaching for him when his eyes riveted to the red splotch spread across her dress.

"Jo—what—are you—?"

She followed his gaze and noticed the stain for the first time. "Cocktail sauce."

Cam sagged with relief.

"Where were you?" Steve was looking pointedly at the security guard.

"He hit me. Afraid I was down for the count, but I'm all right now." All business, he knelt over the gunman. "Cahill's going to make it. But he's through harassing you."

"Good." Jo stared at the man sprawled on the floor. The attack had happened so fast. Her brain was just starting to catch up with the action. After Eddie Cahill had killed his wife, he'd been waiting for his opportunity to ambush her. The excitement of the wedding reception had given him the perfect chance.

The wedding! This was happening in the middle of Steve and Abby's wedding reception. Jo felt her face heat as she shot the tuxedo-clad groom a mortified glance. "I'm making a shambles of your big day," she muttered.

"Don't be ridiculous." Steve didn't miss a beat. "You've just livened up the occasion. The important thing is that the two of you are all right."

Jo looked at Cam. "You know, I was really looking forward to the shrimp. Too bad, I'm wearing them and the sauce."

"Damn! Another missed opportunity to field test my spot remover," he struggled to match her ironic tone.

A blond waiter pushed his way through to the front of the crowd that had gathered around them. Jo remembered him from the reception Abby's mother had given.

"Let me give you a hand," he offered kindly. "I think I've got something that will take that stain out."

"Thanks."

She was about to follow him out of the room when Cam reached toward her. They clenched hands, and for several heartbeats she was caught up in the sensation of his strong fingers gripping hers.

Oh, Cam, don't ever let me go again.

"Come on. You want to get back to the party," the waiter urged.

"Yes. Right." Jo allowed herself to be led away, conscious of the tight hold on her arm. The man was gripping her as forcefully as Cam had. At the door, she hesitated.

"I'll meet you back here," Cam told her, and she knew that before they returned to the reception they were going to settle their own unfinished business.

"Yes."

The waiter gave her a little tug. "Hurry. Before the stain sets."

She nodded, vaguely confused and uneasy. Something was wrong. Something— But the experience she'd just been through had robbed her of the ability to think clearly.

They headed down the hall toward the employees' washroom.

"What's your name?" She tried to start a conversation.

"Art."

"I guess the staff has to be equipped for anything."

"That's right. I'm equipped for anything."

In the next moment she felt cold metal against her ribs.

"This time it's not your friend Rossini playing jokes. I've got a gun. Bring your hands together behind your back."

Jo briefly considered bolting—or screaming. The menacing jab of the gun against her side convinced her it was safer to play along. Seconds after she'd complied with the order, she felt metal cuffs clamp around her wrists. They were hidden from view by the man in back of her.

Panic welled up in her throat as she tried to shift her hands. Her chances of escape had just dwindled to near zero.

"Move it." Then he was shoving her through a door and into the parking lot.

Jo's mind scrambled for sanity—for rational explanations. Was this an accomplice of Eddie?

She stumbled. The man with the gun cursed as he jostled her down the sidewalk.

They were almost to a gray van. Panic and little flashes of mental clarity pinged through her mind with lightning speed. He was going to shove her inside and drive away. When he did, no one would know what had happened to her.

Was there anything she could drop? Some clue she could leave? Not with her hands manacled behind her back.

What about her shoe? No, he'd see it. Then she remembered the gold band that was still on her right hand. With her thumb, she worked it down her finger. As it dropped she held her breath. It didn't hit the concrete and give her away. It was on the grass.

The door of the van slid open. Once Jo was inside, her kidnapper's tense expression changed to one of confidence. As he secured the manacle to a ring riveted into the wall, a little giggle escaped from his lips. Her heart froze. She recognized the sound. The man on the phone! The man who had told her exactly what he was going to do to her.

A scream tore from her lips as the van pulled out of the parking lot.

ABBY, WHO HAD GONE searching for her new husband, joined the group in the kitchen.

"What happened?" she asked, aghast as she spotted the wounded man still lying on the floor.

"Eddie Cahill, the escaped drug dealer who was after Jo," Steve explained. "He's gonna live to serve out the rest of his term. On top of ones for murder and attempted murder."

"Where's Jo?" The bride's voice was still anxious.

"Cleaning up." Cam gestured toward the mess on the floor. "I'm afraid Cahill turned the kitchen into a giant shrimp cocktail."

Abby lifted her white dress away from the ruined party food, and Steve slung his arm around her shoulder.

As the groom recounted the action for the bride, more and more employees gathered to listen. But Cam hardly paid any attention to the narrative as he kept glancing at the door.

The police came to cart away Eddie Cahill, and he had to answer some questions.

"We'll need to talk to Ms. O'Malley, too."

"She'll be right back."

The minutes stretched.

"Where is she?"

"I'll get her."

Cam went out in the hall and glanced around, fighting the tension knotting his stomach. There was no sign of Jo or the waiter who had hustled her out of the room so quickly.

"Excuse me," he asked one of the passing busboys. "Did you see the maid of honor and one of the waiters?"

"The lady with the big red stain on her dress?"

"Yes."

"They went through there." The boy gestured toward a door and hurried off.

The knot tightened into a strangle-hold as Cam jogged down the hall and pushed open the door. He was only half surprised to find that it led to the parking lot behind the kitchen.

Nothing moved as he walked toward the catering trucks and employee vehicles. Maybe the busboy had been mistaken.

If his head hadn't been bowed in concentration, he would have missed a small piece of metal in the grass. It winked in the sunlight.

Cam stooped to pick it up. Jo's ring. The one she'd never taken off.

Oh, my God! What had happened to her? Clasping the ring in his fist, he dashed back toward the building.

WITH HER HANDS angled in back of her and secured to the wall, every sway of the van sent a painful jolt through Jo's arms and shoulders. And every jolt was like a stab of fear piercing her breast.

Get away. Escape, her mind screamed. *Before he— Before he—*

Physically flight was impossible. The temptation to shut down her mind, to withdraw to a deep, guarded place within herself where she'd be safe was overwhelming.

The vehicle jounced over a bump and a wrenching jolt of pain ricocheted down Jo's arms. It brought her back to reality.

She lifted her head. For the first time since she'd been shoved into the van, she took in her surroundings. The interior was filled with boxes and cartons of wires and circuit boards and tools—along with a small workbench. Racks of electronic equipment lined the walls.

The implications suddenly hit her in the gut like a street fighter's punch. The transmitter Cam had found on her car. The mystery of the malfunctioning garage door opener. The electromagnetic pulse. The television gone haywire. Eddie Cahill hadn't done any of that.

Her eyes shot to the man in the driver's seat. He didn't look back at her. But she could hear him muttering in a low, urgent voice.

The sound was no longer electronically distorted, yet the speech rhythms were the same ones she knew so well from the phone calls.

Now he had her. Just like—just like—Margaret Clement.

No. Oh, God no.

Desperately she wrenched at the ring that bound her to the wall. She was no match for the thick metal.

Instead she forced herself to listen to the words spewing forth from the man driving the van. He was talking to himself. No, he was really talking to her. The same phrases over and over.

"Wedding party... Denise... Maid of honor... Like an angel... Redheaded bitch."

"Denise?" she gasped. "You have the wrong person. Let me go. Please, let me go."

He swiveled around and fixed her with an angry look. "I liked you, you know that? With your short hair and your slim little body, you reminded me of a boy. And I thought I could—I could . . ." His voice trailed off for a moment, and she saw his features tighten. "I could have done it!" he insisted, but there was an undercurrent of uncertainty in the assertion. "I asked you to marry me, and you laughed at me. You shouldn't have laughed, Denise. You shouldn't have laughed because I needed you. You could have saved me. You could have changed my life."

Even as she caught a note of desperation in his tone, Jo cringed away from his piercing stare. "Please, I—I—don't know you," she stammered.

"Sure you do, Denise."

"Please—"

"Don't play games with me, angel face. You'll make me angry."

He turned back to the road.

CAM YANKED at the door that led back into the hallway. It was locked from the inside. He might have gone around to the front of the building, but he wasn't exactly thinking clearly. Raising his fists he began to pound against the metal barrier.

"Okay, keep your pants on," somebody shouted from the other side. Then a man in a white apron threw the door open.

Cam didn't stop to explain. Instead he pushed past him and sprinted down the hall to the employees' washroom. A startled salad girl looked up from the sink and then shrank away as he advanced on her.

"The woman with the stained dress?" he demanded sharply.

"Haven't seen her since she left the kitchen. And I came in here right after that."

She had hardly finished the last sentence before Cam was on his way back to the pantry area. Steve and the security guard were still talking to Abby. He'd been gone for less than five minutes. It just seemed like five hundred. The policeman who'd taken his statement had given up waiting for Jo and started interviewing some of the kitchen help.

"Cam, what's wrong?" Abby gasped when she saw the wild look on his face.

"Jo and that waiter have both disappeared."

"Maybe they're still in the washroom," Abby suggested.

"I checked. They're not there." Cam held up the ring. "I found this outside in the grass beside the parking lot. It's Jo's. It couldn't have slipped off her finger. She had to have taken it off deliberately."

Abby stared at Cam. "But why? The danger's over. You got Eddie."

"Then where's Jo? I think the waiter hustled her down the hall and outside into a car."

Abby gulped. "The phone caller. Jo just about proved it wasn't Eddie."

"The waiter was at the Franklins' house. I remember him because I was thinking he didn't exactly fit in," Steve entered the conversation.

"The maids of honor...the ones Jo talked to..." Abby rambled. "One of them was kidnapped. And she hasn't been heard from again."

Hoping against hope, they dispersed to separate areas of the building to search for Jo. They were joined by the security guard and police officer still on the scene. By the time they'd finished, everyone at the reception had heard about the incident.

The grim news ended the party. The guests departed, leaving the bar fully stocked and buffet table loaded with food. The bride and groom and the best man hardly noticed.

Laura, Lou Rossini, and Noel joined the circle of anxious friends in the kitchen where Cam was drilling the staff. He found out quickly that the waiter's name was Arthur Thorp.

"What do you know about him?" Cam demanded.

Various staff members contributed bits of information, Thorp looked to be in his early thirties. He was a temporary employee of Perfection Catering Service who only worked at peak periods.

Another one of the waiters remembered that he hadn't known the business very well at the beginning. But he'd sure been a handy guy to have around. Several times he'd pulled Perfection's chestnuts out of the fire by stepping in to fix malfunctioning kitchen equipment.

Cam looked up from the middle of the interrogation to find Abby ushering Evan Hamill into the kitchen.

"I decided we need the detective who's been in on the case from the beginning," she explained.

"Yeah," he agreed, his voice grim.

Hamill's arrival put the situation into bleak perspective. Finding Jo wasn't going to be easy. And every second she was missing put her life in greater jeopardy.

Chapter Thirteen

Art opened the door of the van and unfastened the handcuffs from the ring on the wall. Lowering her arms brought a sting of pain to Jo's numb limbs.

She shrank away from his touch as he forced her out of the van. But he kept a firm hold on her biceps as he hurried her through a large garage.

They were parked next to a silver Toyota. He caught her glancing at it.

"Alternative transportation in case anyone's looking for my van," he explained. Then his voice changed as he hustled her past a workbench and machine tools. "We're going outside for a minute. If you scream, you're dead. Got it?" The gun barrel in her back emphasized the order.

"Yes," Jo whispered.

The air outside was cold and raw. It was a tantalizing hint of freedom that was quickly squelched as Jo's captor bustled her into a backyard full of weeds and screened with unclipped privet hedges. Jaunty music floated toward her on the wind. Something strident and jarring would have been more appropriate.

The upbeat tune persisted. It was being played by a band. The same one that she'd heard in the background on several of the phone calls.

She was ushered quickly up rickety steps that led to a back porch. Her kidnapper paused to turn off a sophisticated security system that looked out of place in its seedy surroundings. A Randolph deluxe model, Jo thought.

The house was about the same vintage as her own Roland Park home, but no one had kept up the interior. In the dim light, she could see that the wood floors were unpolished and uneven, old wallpaper hung down in yellowing strips in several places, and cobwebs festooned every corner. The air of mustiness made it hard to take a deep breath.

The whole effect made Jo feel closed-in and queasy. She fought back her revulsion and ordered her detective's mind to store as many details as possible.

When she lingered, her captor gave her a shove down the hall. It was lined with several closed doors. He directed her toward the second one on the right. She breathed a sigh of relief when she saw he wasn't taking her upstairs where she'd have to climb down a drainpipe or something to get away. She stopped short when she saw the door was guarded by a separate security monitor.

Taking her arm, Art jostled her inside where she squinted in the bright light that contrasted so sharply with the rest of the interior.

He pushed her toward a narrow bed lined up against one wall. At least it wasn't *the* bed, the brass one in the video. But a ring and a chain dangled from the wall.

"Please..." Jo didn't try to keep the quaver out of her voice. Maybe if she played on his sympathy. "Please, my arms hurt so much. Don't chain me."

Art laughed. "You expect me to trust you? The day I snatched your purse, you kicked me."

"You—" The revelation numbed her to the bone.

"Sit down," he ordered.

Jo's glance flitted to the bed, which was covered with a homespun quilt, and then back to the gun trained on her chest.

Her captor followed her gaze. "I don't want to shoot you, but I will if I have to," he growled.

She sat gingerly on the very edge of the bed while he secured one hand to a cuff that dangled from a chain attached to the wall.

When he was finished, he stood over her for endless moments contemplating her slender frame. Jo steeled herself to keep from quaking like a sapling in a windstorm. She didn't raise her gaze to meet his. She didn't want him to see the horror in her eyes.

Now that he was completely in control, his voice took on a subtle note of satisfaction. "I worked hard to get things ready for you."

Crossing to the closet, he opened the door. Like a mouse dropped into a cage with a snake, Jo fought paralysis as she followed his movements.

When he brought out several garments on hangers, she gasped in surprise. Two of them were the suit and apricot cocktail dress that had disappeared from the cleaners. The others were slacks and blouses he'd stolen from her closet the night he'd rigged the television set.

There were other personal things, too, she saw, as she looked around the room. Novels that she'd read were on the bedside table. The lipstick from her purse was on the dresser, along with a number of the toilet articles she used. And then there was the quilt, so much like the one on her own bed at home.

Such simple, everyday objects. Yet because they were here in this room, terror threatened to carry her away in its undertow.

The room was like a carefully constructed stage setting. Unreal, yet with the appearance of reality. What drama was going to be enacted? She was pretty sure she knew what the director had in mind for the finale. Her only chance was to change the script.

"For dinner, I'll fix you some of your favorite foods. I looked in your trash and found out the kind of stuff you like to cook."

He'd been spying on her for weeks, collecting her things, dogging her every move. He'd even pawed through her trash! Nausea warred with terror.

Then she realized he might have made a fatal mistake. Her trash. If it was after the camera—No, she was grasping at straws. But if he had—If he had— Jo tried to keep any hint of hope out of her voice. "You know so much about me," she whispered instead. "You must know who I am. I'm Jo O'Malley. I'm not the woman who hurt you. I'm not Denise."

"Shut up!"

Jo nodded. *Careful,* she warned herself. *You just made a mistake.*

"Denise," he repeated, staring at her, his eyes slightly out of focus. "Denise. You were going to make an honest man of me. And then you slapped me. You shouldn't have done that. Do you understand?"

"Yes," Jo whispered. She fought to keep her teeth from chattering and her body from trembling. The man who had her in his clutches was stark-raving mad. Anything could set him off.

His eyes seemed to snap back into focus. "You're Jo O'Malley. But you look like Denise. You're playing her role in the wedding. You'll do fine as her stand-in. Only this time, things are going to come out differently.

Her control cracked. "You can't get away with this. The police will catch you."

"No they won't. The police can't trace the phone calls. And they don't know who I am." He giggled and reached up to his full head of blond hair. "You thought you were so clever with your costumes. Mine are better." With a deft motion, he tugged at the covering. It was a wig, and it came away in his hand to reveal stringy brown hair.

Jo couldn't stifle a tiny exclamation. He grinned at her as he tossed the wig into the trash can. "The punk hairdo was another one of my disguises," he boasted. Crossing to the mirror he pulled a layer of rubber makeup away from one cheek and then from the other. More rubber came off his nose. "Good stuff," he commented. "I should have used it that day in Dundalk. But I didn't think you were going to claw my face."

Jo watched the skinlike appliances follow the wig into the trash. She hadn't spotted the camouflage.

"No more Art Thorp," he said airily. "After this, I'll have to build up another persona. Get a job at another catering company."

"Art Thorp?"

"That's who they think I am." He giggled again. "They don't know anything about the real me. Art Nugent." He was still speaking into the mirror, suddenly he turned and faced Jo again. "I've been waiting for weeks to tell you all this," he crowed.

"You know so much. Like the stuff you told me on the phone. About Cam."

"I just pointed you toward the files."

"That wasn't a lucky guess. You have inside information."

"Yes!"

The way he said the word brought a choking feeling to Jo's chest. But she kept up the game.

"I was impressed."

He took a step forward, and she thought again about all the sexual references he'd made in those tapes. She backed up on the narrow bed and found her shoulders pressed against the wall.

He smiled. But only with his lips, not his eyes. "You don't like me any more than Denise did. She was just pretending to be nice. Until the wedding was over."

"That's not true. I do like you."

"I know what you're trying to do with your clever little conversation. You're trying to feed my ego—and get information. It won't make any difference what you do. I have you, and Cameron Randolph doesn't. I keep wondering, was it chance or fate that paired you with Randolph that night of the Franklin party?"

"Why do you care so much about Cam?"

"Your boyfriend is that inventor bastard who thinks he's the king of Randolph Enterprises. The man who wouldn't let me into the design department, even after Collin recommended me. His majesty Cameron Randolph still thought I wasn't good enough. Well, I was. And I paid him back." He couldn't repress one of the giggles that had made her skin crawl when he'd talked to her on the phone. Only now they were in the same room. "Too bad Skip O'Malley isn't around to sweat out where you are. I beat him once, but I can't touch him now. I can only make sure Randolph pays.''

At that moment, Jo was too stunned to reply. Later she thought about good and bad luck—and what it meant to her that Art Nugent chose that moment to turn and bolt from the room.

GOOD AND BAD LUCK. Was this all going to hinge on good and bad luck, Cam wondered as he sat before his computer, which was swiftly running through number and letter combinations.

As the digits flashed on the screen, he took off his glasses and rubbed the bridge of his nose. He looked like a man who had gone ten rounds with Mike Tyson. Then he shook his head and roused himself from the dark mood.

You're going to make it, Jo. We'll find you. It's going to be all right, he prayed. He had to believe that. Because if they didn't, there was no more meaning to his life.

The door opened behind him, and he looked around expectantly. It was Abby. Silently she shook her head, and he turned quickly back to the screen so that she wouldn't see the raw disappointment on his face.

He, Laura, Abby, Steve and Noel had established a command post at his town house. Most of them were still out checking various leads and looking for clues they might have missed at Jo's house or office. He was manning the computer link to the police department and doing his own checking of data bases.

''You and Steve should be off on your honeymoon,'' he said in a low voice.

''You don't really think we could leave now, do you?''

"I wasn't suggesting that you go. I'm just trying to tell you I feel guilty."

"Don't."

"If I'd been straight with her, this wouldn't have happened."

"The man who grabbed her had every detail planned. He would have gotten to her anyway."

Cam had been over all the arguments with himself. Why punish Abby by continuing the discussion with her? He glanced at the screen. The program didn't need any help from him at this point, so that his mind was free to rehash the events of the past few hours.

There had been no problem convincing Hamill or the Baltimore County police that Jo's life was in jeopardy. Cam had been amazed at the way the detective had cut through red tape that would have tied another man's hands for days. Because the Social Security Administration was in Baltimore, Hamill had worked personally with a number of executives in the government agency. One of them agreed to go down to the office and check out Art Thorp, even though it was Saturday afternoon. He called back with the news that an area man named Art Thorp had applied for a social security number three years ago. Regular deposits had been made into his account since then by employers.

The recent vintage of the account almost certainly meant the kidnapper was using an assumed name. And the address on file was a town house in Camden occupied by a young couple who knew nothing about a man named Art Thorp.

The information from the Social Security Administration led nowhere. Also, Thorp's personnel file had disappeared from the catering office, and his phone number had been pulled from the office Rolodex. On the other hand, a number of the employees at the catering service remembered Art Thorp's gray van—which had been parked near the entrance through which Jo had been hustled out of the building. Thorp had been very secretive about what was inside. When another waiter had recently asked him for a ride to the bus stop because his car was in the shop, Thorp had made what sounded like a flimsy excuse not to grant the small favor.

The incident in itself wouldn't have been significant, except that the waiter remembered looking at the license plate on the van. Although he didn't recall the whole number-letter combination, he was sure that the last two digits were 64—because that was the year he'd been born.

Hamill had arranged for the Randolph Enterprise computer system to access the records at the Motor Vehicles Administration. Cam was now laboriously searching the data base, looking for vehicles with that particular combination in the last two positions. There were thousands. Which meant they needed to eliminate most of the tags from the list.

Abby came up behind Cam again and stood watching the numbers moving across the screen. "You must be tired."

"I'm all right."

"Want some dinner? I brought some food back from the reception. I figured we might as well eat it."

"Maybe later."

Abby reached out and began to knead the tense muscles of his shoulders.

Cam sighed. "That feels good. But what would your fiancé think if he came in right now?"

"Her husband, buddy. He's her husband." Steve regarded them from the doorway. He'd come in quietly and chosen to wait for the right moment to make his presence known.

"Luckily he knows you're just good friends," Steve continued. "Otherwise, he'd break a few important bones in your body. Besides, you've got a girl of your own. As soon as we get her back, she can take over the R and R duties."

Jo sat staring at the closed door, feeling Art's presence on the other side. Her ears detected tiny clicks as he set the security alarm.

She raised her hand and looked at the metal chain and cuff. Medieval technology. But the security system was state-of-the-art. Her captor was covering all the bases. At least she hadn't given him another advantage by blurting the first thing that had sprung to her tongue when he'd mentioned Cam and Skip.

But how did you act with a lunatic? How did you keep from setting him off? His grip on reality was so fragile. Sometimes he didn't even know who she was.

Denise. Margaret. Jo.

The depth of Nugent's insanity brought a wave of cold sweat sweeping across her body. Then, by brute force, she pulled her mind back from the brink of its own destruction. Maybe his previous victims had simply given up. She wasn't going to do that.

She had too much to live for. *Cam. Oh, Cam,* she thought. *I'm coming back to you.*

For precious moments she let her lids flutter closed and allowed herself to think about him. How it had been in his arms. How it would be again. Warm. Loved. Cherished. Everything she'd secretly longed for but hadn't dared seek.

At first in the fantasy, he simply held her and told her over and over that everything was going to be all right. But as she clung to him, he began to talk to her in a low, urgent voice.

"Use what he said to you. He's given you some clues. Some important information."

"Yes!"

Deliberately she focused on Art Nugent's mad babblings.

He'd worked for Randolph Electronics, gotten angry and paid Cam back for not letting him into the design department. He talked as if he hated Cam. Could she use that? How? She had to think of a plan.

Jo glanced at the closed door again. How long did she have before he came back? And what could she accomplish in his absence?

Methodically, as if she were going over a crime scene for clues, Jo began to inspect her surroundings. The first thing she determined was that the security system covered the window as well as the door.

Next she began to inspect the bed. It was made of iron and bolted to the floor. The ring that attached her chain to the wall seemed solidly mounted. Perhaps she could find some tool to pry it loose.

The length of the chain was also of considerable interest. It allowed her to move a few feet away from the bed. She could reach the dresser. Hopefully there was something in one of the drawers that would be useful.

She had gotten up when a noise in the hall stopped her in her tracks. The realization that her captor was coming back was like a blast of frigid air against her skin, and she wrapped her arms around her shoulders. What was his timetable? How fast did he plan to move? What she needed was to buy herself some time.

Buy some time! The phrase triggered an idea—the plan she'd been searching for began to jell.

Do it right, she warned herself. *Don't let him catch on to what you're trying to pull.*

THERE WAS STILL no way to narrow down the thousands of license numbers flagged by Cam's computer program. The police didn't have a clue about the real identity of the man holding Jo. And Cam felt as if the seconds of her life were ticking by.

Abby had gone off to interview some of the other women from the phone company list.

Laura still hadn't come back from Jo's office.

Cam wandered into the den, sat down on the sofa and began to fiddle with the stereo system. The last time Jo had been here, they'd listened to Kenny Rogers.

He found the compact disc and began to play it again, unable to hold back the wave of longing for Jo that would have knocked him off his feet if he'd been standing up.

You'll be here with me again, he promised silently. *Safe and sound. Then I'll tell you all the things I was going to say when Cahill burst into the kitchen.*

He'd thought the music would make him feel closer to her. It only made things worse.

Getting up again, he went back to his home office. Hamill had dropped off the tapes from Jo's answering machine. Maybe if he played them, he'd get some clue.

There was nothing useful, but because he'd just been listening to music, the faint tune in the background caught his attention. The police had told them the notes were too distorted to recapture. But his equipment was probably better than theirs. If he ran the recording through his computer, he could bring the tune into sharper focus. Picking up the tapes, he started for his electronics workshop.

It took several hours of fiddling, but Cam finally got an acceptable rendition of the music. It sounded like a college football song, but sports had never been one of his big interests.

Had Art Thorp, or whatever his name was, been watching the game of the week when he'd made the call? That seemed unlikely.

People had come in and out of the house while he'd been working but no one had disturbed him. But when Laura wandered back to see what he was doing, the music made her linger in the doorway.

"Why are you playing that?" she asked.

He turned bloodshot eyes toward her. "You don't recognize it, do you?"

"Of course I recognize it. It's 'Stand up Towson.'"

"What?"

She sang a few bars. "'Stand up Towson, Stand up Towson, Strike that note of fame.' It's my old high-school song. Why are you playing it?"

"You never heard the tapes?"

"Tapes?" She looked puzzled for a moment. "You mean the ones Jo got."

There was a note of excitement in his voice. "Yes. The song was in the background, but until I enhanced it, it was too faint to identify." He rewound the cassette and played it again. At one point the music stopped, backed up several bars, and started again. Later the drum was definitely out of synch with the rest of the instruments.

"It sounds like the band practicing," Laura mused.

"Which means that the place he was calling from must be within hailing range of the high-school football field."

Cam pointed to the computer terminal, which was networked to the one in his office. "I've been racking my brain trying to figure out a way to narrow down the set of license numbers from the DMV. And you've just handed it to me. Where is Towson High School?"

"Off York Road. Near the Towson State University."

Cam brought up a gridded map of Baltimore County on the screen and zoomed in on the area around the school. "Right here." He pointed at the screen. "The bastard was right around here when he made two of those calls. Let's hope he still is."

AS THE DOORKNOB turned, Jo schooled her features to match the role she needed to play.

Art was carrying a tray. The pinched look on his face, the spacey expression in his eyes told her that his hold on reality was slipping.

"Macaroni and cheese," he announced in a cheery voice that didn't sound as if it were coming from his lips. He set the tray down on the stand beside the bed. "One of your favorites."

Jo peered at the goopy, overcooked mess and pictured it sticking to the roof of her mouth. But she dutifully sat down on the edge of the bed and picked up the fork in her unbound hand. *Better follow directions. Better act as if you're eager to do what he says.*

A glass of Coke and a brownie completed the menu. As soon as she got home, she'd have to start eating better, Jo told herself. And she would get home, she added.

"So how long have you lived here?" she asked in a conversational tone.

"I grew up here. I kept the house after my parents died."

"Oh."

"Don't you like your dinner?" He sat down in the overstuffed chair across from the bed.

"Oh, yes, it's very good. I just can't eat very fast," she murmured.

"You need to keep your strength up. We're going to have a very special time together, Denise. It's going to be the way it should have been all along." He was looking at her again in that strange, unfocused way. The tone of his voice was suddenly leaden with grief. "I killed a man, you know. He was my best friend."

"What?"

"It was an accident. Please. You have to believe me. I didn't mean for it to happen."

"I believe you."

"He just got caught in—in—the investigation. And he didn't know what else to do." Art buried his head in his hands for long seconds.

Jo hardly dared breath, wondering what this erratic madman would do next.

When he looked back up at her, his eyes were bright. "I was a lost soul. Damned to hell for everything I'd done. Then I met you. That day when I saw you standing there in church, I thought you were my salvation. You were an angel come to save me, Denise. Angel face, I called you. You were going to change my destiny. Make everything different. Make me pure and whole again."

"I will make you whole again. Just tell me what to do," she whispered.

"You had your chance. Now it's too late for you to do it on your own. I'm the one in charge."

Oh, God. He was so mixed up. Angels. Salvation. Destiny. Could she get him to remember who she really was—to think about her and Cam, again.

"You're such a good engineer," she said softly. "Cameron Randolph should have let you work in the design department."

"Yes!" His face reformed into a mask of anger.

"And now you're going to get even with him," Jo continued. "You're going to use me to get money out of Cam, aren't you?" she asked in a small, trembly voice.

The room grew very still. Jo didn't dare glance up. Instead she pushed a clump of macaroni and cheese around the plate.

"Yeah, that's right," Art finally said. "Your boyfriend is worth millions, and I'm going to get some of that undeserved cash away from him."

Jo was positive he hadn't thought of the idea until now. He'd been too focused on Denise being his salvation and how she'd betrayed him. "You're going to trade me for the money," Jo stated as if the assumption were fact.

He looked at her consideringly. "That depends on how you treat me, angel face. Maybe I'm going to get the money and keep you."

"The money is the important thing."

"No. The important thing is our relationship."

Jo held her breath.

"Denise wouldn't marry me. She wouldn't save me. Denise—" He stopped abruptly and stared at her face. "But you will."

The words and the way he was looking at her made a tide of nausea rise in her throat. What did she have to do to save him? She wanted to scream out her denial. It was all a mistake. He had the wrong woman. She was mixed up in his madness—and some fantasy he'd conjured up about salvation for his sins.

She hadn't really expected him to jump at the idea of letting her go. But collecting a ransom took time.

He got slowly out of the chair, and she stopped breathing.

"I'm going out for a while. When I come back, you can practice being nice to me," he said in a chatty voice as though the whole previous conversation had never existed.

Jo felt a mixture of elation and revulsion.

Time. He'd just given her some time. But then what?

Chapter Fourteen

Cam looked at the salmon pâté from the reception and thought that if he tried to swallow a bite, it would stick to the roof of his mouth. None of the food on the kitchen table held much appeal—to him or anyone else. Even Hamill had given up his smokehouse almonds.

Everyone except the detective from Baltimore County who'd recently joined the task force looked dead tired. But no one seemed inclined to go to bed—except Laura who'd excused herself an hour ago.

When the phone rang, Cam listlessly crossed the room and picked up the receiver.

"Hello?"

"I have your girlfriend." It was the same electronically distorted voice he'd come to know so well.

Fatigue rolled off him like water after a rainstorm. He stood up straighter. He'd never handled a call like this, but he'd better get it right. "Who's calling? Where's Jo? Is she all right?"

The voice on the other end of the line ignored all but the middle question. "It's going to cost you a million bucks to find out."

"That's a lot of money."

Cam glanced toward the table. Everybody was watching him, their tension mirroring his own.

"Don't you think little Ms. O'Malley's worth it?" the caller prodded. "She sure is hot in bed."

"You bastard."

"Now now. You have to learn to share. I expect to have the money in small bills tomorrow."

"Nobody can raise a million dollars that fast."

"You'd better try."

"You'd better prove to me that Jo is alive before I pay out anything. I want to talk to her."

"That's impossible."

"I'll pay the money, but only if I can be sure of what I'm getting."

"I'll think about it," the voice rasped.

The line went dead.

"I'll tell you where the call was made in a minute," Hamill said.

"Oh God, he said he raped her."

Abby got up and put her arm around Cam's shoulder. "He could be lying to get a rise out of you."

He tried to comfort himself with that.

"I wasn't sure what to say. I didn't expect him to contact me."

"The most important thing is that he's changed his pattern. He's never asked for a ransom before—which means it was probably Jo's idea."

"She's manipulating him?"

"Yes."

"Then she must be . . . okay."

"Yes."

He felt the two-ton weight pressing against his chest ease up an inch or two.

Hamill joined the conversation again. "Another phone booth. In a shopping center north of the city."

"Not far from Towson?"

"Right. I've got every patrol car in the area looking for a van with those last two numbers on the license plate."

"We'll catch him," Abby cut in.

Cam didn't answer. Instead he reached for the phone again.

"Who are you calling?" Steve asked.

"My bank. I'll have to cash in some securities."

"You can't call the bank. It's closed."

Cam blinked. He hadn't been thinking about the time or the day of the week. All he'd been thinking about was Jo.

"He's not going to exchange Ms. O'Malley for the money," Hamill said in a quiet voice.

"I'm going to have to operate under the assumption that he will."

ART HAD BEEN GONE for over an hour. Jo hadn't wasted a moment of the reprieve. As soon as he'd closed the door and set the security lock, she'd pushed away the food and taken a good look at the arrangement that held her chain to the wall. A round metal ring similar to the type used to cover a plumbing pipe hid the attachment. Jo couldn't remove it with her hands so she went looking for a tool. It wasn't too difficult to pry off a metal corner brace from the bottom of the bed. With it she carefully pulled up the ring. Underneath she could see that a bolt had been cemented into the wall.

Experimentally she began to work at the cement with the corner brace. It yielded to her efforts, but it was going to be slow work. What if her captor discovered what she was doing? The speculation made her go momentarily numb. What would he do if she didn't get away?

Slipping the ring back against the wall, she saw that it would hide her handiwork as effectively as it had hidden the connection. If Art didn't lift up the covering, she'd be all right. Except that chipping away at cement was going to create dust and other debris. A dead giveaway. She'd have to contain the mess.

In the middle dresser drawer, she found one of her T-shirts. Spreading it out along the edge of the bed, she began to chisel at the cement. It was slow going. She forced herself to get up periodically, empty the dust into the bottom dresser drawer, and cover the evidence with the remaining pieces of clothing.

While she worked, she imagined Cam there beside her. Encouraging her. Telling her that she could get away.

Conjuring up his image again helped more than she would have believed possible.

She kept her ears tuned for outside sounds. But in her mind, as her hands worked, she was continuing the silent dialogue she'd started with Cam.

"In the van, he said I reminded him of a boy. But that he couldn't—"

"That makes it sound like he's gay."

"Yes!" Her heart began to thump. "All those sexual threats—he just wants to talk about sex with women. He won't actually follow through." She prayed it was true.

Her hand chipped away at the cement. Her mind kept up the internal dialogue.

"He said he worked at Randolph Enterprises and you wouldn't let him in the design department. He said he killed his best friend—but it was an accident."

"Collin?"

"Maybe Collin tried to get him the job because the two of them were involved. Maybe that's how he got the designs, too. It fits what we know. Your brother killed himself after he found out someone he trusted was responsible for the industrial espionage.

"Cam, I'm scared. He's so crazy." Jo had been fighting to keep her thoughts on a logical, rational level. Now she stopped chipping at the cement and let out the little whimper she'd been holding in.

"Honey, I know you're afraid. But we're going to get through this," Cam whispered reassuringly in her mind. Jo swallowed and went on with the silent speculation. "Probably he was pretty unstable—but he managed to hide it. Collin's suicide tipped the balance. It drove him insane because he couldn't cope with what he'd done."

"Yes. Suppose he's one of those gay men who never came to terms with his sexual identity? Maybe he'd sworn to himself that he was going to turn over a new leaf after his lover died. He told me Denise looked like an angel come to save him. In his crazed mind, he pinned all his hopes on her. Then she rejected him."

"I'll bet she was afraid of the madness in him as much as anything else. Maybe he was already so far gone that he started babbling to her about angels and lost souls and damnation."

"Maybe."

"The important thing is that when she turned him away, she confirmed his worst feelings about himself."

"He punished her for that. And he's kept on punishing her—through women who looked like her and who were playing the same role."

It all made a kind of terrible sense. Jo went over it again, refining the theory and thinking about how to use what she'd figured out as she worked on freeing herself.

What if she could convince Art she was really his savior? Would he let his guard down? Unchain her? Or was he too far gone for that?

When she heard the back door to the house open, every muscle in her body tensed. Fearfully she looked down at the pile of cement dust. Not much!

With rapid, jerky motions, Jo pushed the ring back into place, folded the mess into the T-shirt, and shoved it under the edge of the mattress. Her improvised tool followed.

As she looked wildly around, she saw that a few flakes of cement remained. She was just sweeping them away as heavy footsteps came down the hall. The security alarm gave her a few extra seconds.

Heart pounding, Jo smoothed out the quilt, flopped back against the wall, and struck an attitude with head bowed as if she'd been sitting in defeat the whole time Art had been gone. Silently she prayed that he wouldn't figure out what she'd been doing.

He opened the door and stood studying her for several moments.

"Your boyfriend isn't sure he wants to pay to get you back," he finally said, his voice rising on a taunting note.

She kept her expression blank.

"I told him you were great in bed."

She couldn't hold back a choked little sound.

Her captor stared at her for endless seconds, his tongue sweeping across his lips. "Maybe we'll find out about that later. Right now Randolph wants me to prove that you're still breathing before he coughs up the cash. How did you meet him, Denise?" He looked puzzled.

"I—uh—"

His expression brightened. "At that party. It was my lucky day when you met at the party."

"Yes. Please, let me talk to him," she begged.

"Not a chance. You might give something away."

"You could make a recording and play it."

She could see he was considering the idea.

"I'll write the message and you can read it over before I make the tape. It will be a lot more persuasive if it's in my own words like the interview in the paper. Remember, you read it?"

He nodded slowly.

"We're going to get married so I can be your savior. But we need to start off with a nest egg," she tossed out casually. She sat as still as a nun in prayer while he considered the proposal.

"All right," he finally agreed.

Did he believe her? Or was he playing his own game?

"If you try any tricks, I'll slit your throat. And I won't wait for the ceremony."

Jo tried to swallow. Her throat felt scorched. "No tricks," she managed.

"I'll get you a pencil and paper."

For once, she was glad that her captor came back so quickly.

"Here." He handed her the writing materials.

"Thank you," she whispered, almost overwhelmed by the chance to communicate with Cam. But she couldn't let Nugent realize how much it meant to her.

Oh, Cam, she thought, blinking back the moisture that filmed her eyes. *When I'm alone, I can pretend you're here. But there's so much I want to say—need to say—to you in person. He's letting me send you a short message, but it won't really be personal. I want to tell you I love you. I can't do that. What I say has to be just the right words. It has to say what Nugent wants—and give you a clue to help you find me.*

"I'M SORRY to bother you. Phil Mercer says he wants to talk to you," Abby interrupted Cam's reveries. He'd been sitting at the computer pretending he was having a conversation with Jo.

Without turning, Cam snapped out an answer. "I told him he was in complete charge at Randolph for the time being. I don't want to be bothered with any details."

"He says it's important."

Sighing, the inventor got up, stretched cramped muscles, and reached for the phone.

"He's not calling. He's in the living room."

Cam didn't bother to mask his surprise as he started for the door.

The Randolph CEO stood by the window. The thinning hair on his round head was mussed, as if he'd run his fingers through it repeatedly. His normally ruddy complexion was tinged with gray. A manila folder that hadn't been there before lay in the middle of the coffee table.

"What brings you out here?" Cam asked.

"The two of us haven't always seen eye to eye on policy at Randolph."

Cam acknowledged the observation with a slight inclination of his head.

"I've tried to keep things running smoothly. Then this terrible business with Ms. O'Malley made me—" He stopped and started again. "Remember a couple of weeks ago when someone used that EMP generator against her, and you had me checking our records?"

Cam nodded.

"When Collin and your father died, you were pretty upset. I decided you wouldn't want to rake all that up again—"

"For God sakes, man, stop stuttering and spit it out."

"Your brother Collin requested copies of the EMP files. He had them for several weeks before they went into inactive storage."

"Collin?"

"It was his signature on the request." Mercer gestured toward the folder on the table.

Cam snatched it up and flipped through the contents. "This request form?" he asked, shoving a piece of paper toward Mercer.

"Yes."

"I know my brother's signature," Cam said in a deceptively quiet voice. "This isn't it."

"But—"

"Someone forged his name."

"Cam, are you sure?" Abby interjected from where she stood in the doorway.

He whipped around to face her. "You think I'm still not able to deal with it, don't you?"

"I just want you to admit the possibility your brother was involved."

He snapped the folder closed and stalked past Abby out of the room with the papers clutched in stiff fingers.

"Cam—wait."

"I'm not going off to sulk," he said in a strained voice. "I'm going off to think."

It wasn't exactly the truth. But it was as close as he could come at the moment.

Like a man walking some grim last mile, Cam climbed the stairs to the attic. With the same solemn determination, he brought down the boxes of Collin's papers that he hadn't looked at in three years.

He hadn't been capable of sorting through them after his brother's death. Now he knew he had to face the truths he wanted to deny.

Was the man who had kidnapped Jo linked to the stolen designs, the EMP generator, Collin's secret relationships? Cam was afraid he already knew the answer. But he'd been too stubborn to listen when Jo had waved the evidence in his face.

With his lips pressed together in a tight line, he tackled the contents of the boxes. The first one contained greeting cards Collin had saved over the years. As he looked through them, he remembered some of their good times—birthdays and Easters and Valentine's Days.

Another box held old school papers. He didn't bother with those.

The next was full of work Collin had brought from Randolph Enterprises to his home office from time to time. It was all pretty predictable, until he got to a sealed manila envelope buried underneath a stack of interoffice memos.

Inside were photocopies of requests for various project specs—including a duplicate of the EMP request Mercer had showed him. Why would Collin have that? Or applications for other designs that had turned up in rival product lines? If he'd been stealing from his own company, wouldn't he have wanted to destroy the evidence?

For long moments Cam sat like a man in a trance. Then he flipped to the back of the first request. It bore the same forged signature that he had seen downstairs.

But Collin had known about it. He'd gone to the trouble of collecting the requests. Had someone else and Collin been in on the industrial espionage plot together? Was Collin protecting himself with proof of the forged signatures? Or had his brother finally realized his secret relationships had made him vulnerable?

Cam raised his eyes and stared off into the distance, trying to imagine his brother's sick panic after his conversation with Skip O'Malley. Maybe it had triggered his own investigation. He wanted to believe that. He wasn't sure he could.

Cam's breath was shallow as he sat sifting through the evidence of what had happened at Randolph Enterprises. He hadn't believed Skip. He hadn't listened to what Jo was trying to tell him about his brother because he still hadn't wanted to know the truth.

The guilt was terrible. If he hadn't tried to block out what Jo was saying, maybe she wouldn't be in the clutches of some madman now. With a curse, he flung the papers across the room and buried his head in his hands.

After a long while he stood up and wiped his eyes. Then he gathered up the scattered papers and went down to do everything in his power to repair the damage. He didn't allow himself to wonder if it might be too late. That possibility was too great a threat to his sanity.

He needed hard copy data from the personnel office. He was halfway out the front door when he remembered he couldn't leave the house. He had to stay here in case the kidnapper called.

Jogging back to the living room, he was surprised to see Phil Mercer still there talking in a low voice to Abby. Maybe the man wasn't as emotionless as he'd thought. "Phil, I want you to go to the office and bring me the Randolph personnel files. Everybody who was working for us three years ago."

"You're talking about a lot of files."

"I expect to see a batch of them on my desk in an hour. Then you can go back for more."

TIME HAD BLURRED into a strange distortion of reality. It was the middle of the night. Jo's nerves were raw as she watched Art read the message she had composed for Cam.

I guess you're wondering what's happened to me. Unfortunately, I'm not free to tell you what's going on. Give the man the money. Everything will be all right. Not to worry, Superman. Trust me.

When her captor's eyes narrowed, her heart leaped into her throat. Had he figured out what she was doing? Please, God, don't let him get it, she prayed.

"Why does it say not to worry, Superman?" he demanded.

It's the only personal thing I could say. "That's what I call him. That way he'll know it's really me. It's important for him to believe he's hearing my own words."

She held her breath as Art mulled over her logic.

"Yeah. All right. It's just like that bozo to think of himself as Superman."

Jo bit back any comment.

"What about the last sentence?" Art continued. "Superman's supposed to trust me—not you."

"We can make it trust *him*. You're the one with the power."

"Yeah. Right. That's a lot better."

Jo watched him pull a small recorder out of the canvas bag he'd brought with him. He was in a hurry. Would that make him careless?

Was he going to kill her as soon as he'd proved to Cam that she was alive? Was he going to stop her if she made a small but critical change in the first sentence?

She gripped the edge of the bed with numb fingers as she waited for him to press the button.

Holding the recorder in his lap, he reached into the canvas bag again and pulled out something that looked like a portable microphone. The wire was attached to some device still hidden by the bag.

First he turned on the recorder. Then he lifted the microphone to his lips and spoke.

"Your girlfriend made you a tape."

The words had the familiar high-pitched electronic distortion. Jo gasped and literally jumped several inches off the bed. Over the past few weeks he'd sensitized her to that unnatural voice like a lover stroking her skin. Again, she felt a cloud of mechanical insects skittering over her body. Frantically her hands tried to brush them away.

When Art saw her reaction, he laughed into the microphone. It was all she could do to keep from screaming.

She had to get a grip on herself. Wrapping her arms around her shoulders, she hugged herself tightly and rocked back and forth.

He thrust the microphone toward her. Your turn, he mouthed.

"Now—now—I guess you're wondering what's happened to me..."

Her voice was unsteady when she began to talk. It gained strength as she read the message she'd composed for Cam.

IT WAS FIVE in the morning. Cam's compulsively neat work area was littered with hundreds of haphazardly scattered personnel files. He was looking through the record of every engineer who had worked for the company eight to three years ago—looking for some link to Collin.

We'll find him, Jo, he muttered under his breath. *We'll find him. Just hang on until we find him.*

So far he'd turned up nothing.

Laura Roswell burst into the room. Her eyes were bright with excitement. Cam's gaze fixed on the photograph she was waving in her hand.

"Look at this. Look at this," she shouted, shoving the picture at him.

He held it under the light. It showed a man with stringy hair and an intense face bent over a trash can.

"What the hell—"

"It's him. The guy who has Jo. Don't you see, it's got to be him. He's been following her around—learning about her. He must have gone back some time in the last couple of weeks and looked through Jo's trash." The words tumbled out one after the other. "I didn't want to get your hopes up, so I didn't say anything when I left. A couple of hours ago, I remembered the camera Jo set up to get a picture of those dogs."

Cam studied the face in the photograph. It didn't look familiar. Not even much like the waiter who had abducted Jo. But maybe—

Quickly he began to shuffle files together.

"You take that stack," he directed Laura. "I'll take this one. They've each got a photograph. One of them may be the guy."

Forty-five minutes later, he acknowledged that none of the men looked like the creep at the trash can. He cursed under his breath.

Another desperate lead that hadn't panned out. Like the van. It wasn't registered in the Towson area.

Cam was sitting with his palms pressed against his burning eyelids when the phone rang.

"Your girlfriend made you a tape."

There was no need to explain who was calling. His hand jerked as he activated the ultrasensitive recorder that he'd hooked up to the phone.

There was a pause of several seconds. Then Jo's voice came on the line. It quavered and he pictured her alone with this madman and terrified.

"Now—now—I guess you're wondering what's happened to me."

Her voice grew in strength and confidence. *That's it, Jo,* he silently encouraged.

"Unfortunately, I'm not free to tell you what's going on. Give the man the money. Everything will be all right. Not to worry, Superman. Trust him."

The sound of her voice sent little prickles of electricity along his nerve endings.

"Jo!"

"Just a recording, stupid."

"How do I know—"

"You don't. But if you want to see her again, you'll put the money in your car and drive to the big boulders near the science building at Goucher College. Monday evening at five. You'll find further instructions there. If the police are following you, your girlfriend is dead."

Cam tried to imagine the further instructions. They probably included disabling his car phone.

"Wait. What if I can't get the money together that fast?"

"Too bad for Ms. O'Malley."

JO WORKED STEADILY—chipping and gouging and hiding the cement dust. Every few minutes she gave a harsh tug on the chain. It didn't budge. The bolt was deeper in the wall than she'd imagined. There wasn't a chance that she could dig it out in time. But she had to try.

Again she tried to keep her spirits up by thinking of Cam. Of getting back to him. Of how happy they'd both be when he held her in his arms again. Now it was hard to make the fantasy work, and she realized she was losing hope.

Denise. Margaret. Jo.

No, she wasn't going to end up like the other two.

When she heard the outside door open, her hand froze, and she looked down at the pile of cement dust and chips on the T-shirt. More cement dust clung to the front of her ruined dress. She'd forgotten to keep things cleaned up.

Eager footsteps hurried down the hall.

Jo swiped her hand across the front of the dress. Then, as the doorknob turned, she swept the metal brace, T-shirt and cement under the covers.

Arthur Nugent's eyes were bright as he opened the door and stood looking at her with strange possessiveness.

"It's time for the wedding ceremony, Denise."

She didn't bother to tell him she was Jo. What difference would that make now?

"We haven't had our rehearsal dinner yet," she murmured instead.

"Dinner! It's almost morning."

"Please. I'm hungry now. Fix me something special."

He considered the request and then grinned as if pleased with one more opportunity to show his knowledge of her habits. "Biscuits. You like biscuits for breakfast."

"Yes."

"All right. I guess that's fair. It will have to be the kind from the refrigerator."

"That's fine."

"I'll be back in a few minutes. Then Denise and I—I mean you and..." He let the sentence trail off, his eyes looking at her meaningfully.

The second the door closed, Jo pulled out the piece of metal and turned back to the wall. Desperately she began to gouge away at the cement around the bolt. She didn't try to work neatly now. This was her last chance. Either she got it loose, or he came to take her away for the ceremony.

THEY HAD ALL GATHERED around the tape recorder. Cam played the message for the fifth time while he stared at the transcription he'd made.

She'd called him Superman so there was a good chance the message was in her own words. Had she used the recording to send him some information?

Cam tried to focus on the message. He'd always been good at word games—at seeing patterns. Now when Jo's life depended on him, his brain was almost too numb to function.

Doggedly he repeated the words.

"Now I guess you're wondering..." That was a strange way to start off, and not at all like Jo's usual speech patterns. "Unfortunately... Give the man... Everything..."

He looked around the room and knew that everybody else was engaged in the same life or death struggle. Steve was hunched forward with his fists clenched. Laura's eyes were shut in concentration. His friends. Jo's friends. And he'd been riding them unmercifully. When this was over...

He realized his mind was wandering and forced it back to the word puzzle.

For endless minutes there was complete silence.

"Nuget," Abby murmured.

Cam's head swiveled toward her. "What?"

"No. *N-U-G-E-N-T.* If you look at the first letter of each sentence's first word, they spell out "nugent." I thought it was "nuget"—that maybe it meant something."

"Nugent." Cam's mind was racing. He'd seen that word. It was a name. A familiar name. Because—because he'd just read it on one of the Randolph Enterprises personnel files.

Leaping up, he began to scramble through the stacks of folders.

"Nugent. It's a name. There's a guy named Nugent here somewhere," he practically shouted.

The others joined him in the hunt. Steve was the one who pulled out the file.

The guy's picture looked as if it had come from a high-school yearbook. He appeared twenty years younger than the man who'd been caught by the trash can. Which was why Cam had passed right over him without reading the contents of the file. Now he could see a resemblance.

COLD SWEAT broke out on Jo's forehead as she hewed away at the cement. When she stopped to tug at the chain, it moved. It moved! With renewed will, she doubled her efforts.

She could wiggle it back and forth now. If she just had a few more minutes—

She'd been so intent on her task that she hadn't heard the door open.

"You bitch! You lied to me again."

With every ounce of strength she possessed, Jo yanked on the chain. The superhuman effort paid off. The bolt came free of the wall. But she hadn't really expected it to give way. In the next second, she tumbled backward onto the hard wooden floor.

Art tossed away the tray he was holding. As biscuits, jelly and hot coffee crashed against the wall, he was sprinting toward Jo.

He was on her in seconds. With more instinct than finesse, she flailed at him with the chain still attached to her left wrist. He grunted as the end careened into his shoulder.

She didn't have time to draw her arm back for another whack. Cursing, face contorted with rage, he went crazy. His hands came up around her neck, shaking and choking. In blind panic, she struggled and gasped for breath. But her air supply was completely blocked. Blackness rose up to meet her.

ARTHUR NUGENT. Skimming his performance appraisals, Cam understood why he didn't remember the man. As an engineer he'd been mediocre. Yet buried in the middle of the material were several recommendations from Collin. He'd hired Nugent above the objections of a senior manager. Later he'd tried to get him transferred to the design department.

Nugent had quit the company three years ago. Just before Collin had died.

Cam felt a mixture of old sadness and new excitement constrict his chest. He'd been looking for someone like this. Someone with a personal connection to his brother. And Jo had sent him the name.

He flipped to the back for the personal data.

"Six years ago he lived in a town house in Randallstown. He listed his father as the person he wanted notified in case of emergency. His father lives in Towson," he told the circle of waiting faces.

"What's the address?" Abby demanded.

Cam read it aloud.

"That's right in back of Towson High School," Laura confirmed.

JO WAS CONSCIOUS of several sensations. Her neck hurt. Drawing in a breath was like sucking in fire. Firm hands grasped her ankles. The handcuff was gone. She was no longer dressed in the ruined maid of honor dress. Cold stone scraped against her hips.

Cautiously she looked down at her body. She was wearing a white dress now. A thin white dress that would have been more appropriate for June than December. The flimsy fabric had ridden up around her waist as Arthur Nugent dragged her across a stone floor.

She held back the scream of black terror that bubbled in her chest. Instead she willed her body to remain limp and peered at the maniac through a screen of lashes. Let him think she was still unconscious. Above her was a vaulted church ceiling. He'd dragged her to a church? How was that possible?

The ceiling looked like granite. No, it was painted plywood. On either side were stained-glass windows made from heavy panes of plastic. Spotlights behind them made the colors glow.

Around her, recorded organ music floated. The wedding march. She could hear Art muttering the words of the ceremony, his voice high and cracking now, weirdly distorted without the need of the electronic device.

"We have gathered here to give thanks for the gift of marriage and to witness the joining together of Arthur and Denise."

He'd brought Denise here. And Margaret, too.

The scream hovered in her throat now. She refused to give it life.

The chapel was tiny—only two rows of pews and then the altar flanked by white flowers. On a low table covered with white linen, a long knife had been laid out. Behind it loomed the brass bed. The one from the home movie. Jo lost the battle to remain limp. Her body jerked, and a scream tore from her lips.

Arthur turned and cuffed the side of her head, momentarily stunning her again. "Shut up! You're spoiling everything. You tried to trick me," he shrieked. "Now we don't have time to do things right."

As he spoke, he hoisted her onto the bed and dragged her arm toward one of the handcuffs that dangled from the headboard.

When she began to struggle, he climbed on top of her, straddling her writhing body with his legs, pressing her down with his weight. She fought him with every remaining ounce of strength. It wasn't enough. Closer, closer. Her right hand drew inexorably closer to the cuff. If he chained her to the bed, the game was over.

Instead of concentrating on Arthur, she switched her attention to the band of metal. Her fingers scrabbled and slid against the smooth surface. Then, miraculously, she had the thing in her hand. With a little gasp of triumph, she squeezed. The cuff snapped shut around empty air. Her hand was still free.

Arthur howled with rage.

Another cuff dangled from the other side of the headboard. He grasped her left hand and folded the fingers closed in a painful grip. Then he began to repeat the process that had just failed.

Somewhere above the music she thought she heard a shout and then an alarm bell clanging. The security alarm. No. It was probably a fantasy. A last desperate rescue fantasy. Her mind had finally provided her with the only escape route possible.

In the next second she was slammed back to reality. Her world had narrowed to the man on top of her dragging her fist toward the handcuff. This time she couldn't close the metal band. This time he had her.

Just as the metal touched her flesh, the door burst open.

"Hold it right there, Nugent," a deep voice barked.

She saw the dazed look on her captor's features. He whirled as if to face the police officers spilling into the room. Then he was lunging for the knife.

It was swinging down toward her chest when shots rang out and he fell backward onto the stone floor.

Chapter Fifteen

Hamill had tried to keep him from joining the rescue operation. But Cam hadn't taken no for an answer. The detective had given in, but when they'd arrived at the house, Cam had been held back behind the police vans while a special unit armed with automatic weapons had surrounded the house and broken in.

It was the longest fifteen minutes of his life. Each hammer beat of his heart was an accusation. The more he thought about it, the more he felt his own culpability. *If you'd had the guts to face up to your brother's role in the industrial espionage, this wouldn't have happened to Jo.*

Now he was finally in the house. But he wore his guilt like a coat of nails with the points gouging into his skin. Jo had to be all right. She had to be! Determinedly he pushed his way through the dozen armed men who separated him from the woman he loved.

He could see her now, huddled on the bed in a torn white dress. She was alive. Thank God she was alive! But she was crying quietly.

Everything else faded into the background. The wedding march that was still playing at full volume. The pews that must have been salvaged from an old church, the garish windows, the cloying smell of the gardenias flanking the altar.

He had to step around a pool of blood on the floor where Nugent's body had lain moments earlier. For an instant he was struck with a strange sense of déjà vu. Another killer. Another threat to Jo's life had ended in a very similar fashion. Only this time the man was dead.

He knelt beside the figure huddled on the bed. She looked so young and defenseless. Against the white sheets, her skin was as pale as marble.

"Jo, honey. It's all over."

Even after the torture of the EMP and the television set, she'd held on to some shreds of self-control. Now somehow his words brought a fresh torrent of tears. What had that bastard done to her?

Or was she crying because she didn't want to face him?

"Oh, God, Jo, are you all right?" *Please be all right.*

He reached out and pulled her into his arms. She hid her face against his chest and clutched his arms as she continued to sob into his shirt.

His fingers soothed over her back and shoulders. It was so damn good just to hold her again. "Oh, Jo, Jo. You're safe. Thank God you're safe."

He could sense her struggling for control. "You got here…I'm sorry…I just…" But she couldn't finish the sentence.

"Jo, forgive me."

She didn't answer. Maybe he didn't deserve her forgiveness.

He felt the sobs ebb. She was still trembling. "Cam— please—"

"Anything, honey. Anything."

"Where is he?"

"Dead. He won't hurt you anymore."

He heard her sigh, felt her relax against him. As she began to speak, he knew she'd gotten back some measure of control. "He was so crazy. I never knew what he was going to do. I couldn't be sure he remembered who I was, even."

It was hard to imagine the horror of it.

"Cam, you saved me."

"We got your message."

"Not just the message. I would have cracked up without you. Well—maybe I did. I kept imagining you there with me, encouraging me, telling me I was going to make it."

"Oh, Jo, honey. I kept thinking those things. Maybe you read my mind."

But as he held her and stroked her and talked softly to her, they both silently admitted that they hadn't been sure they would see each other again.

"I'd like to examine her," a police doctor broke into their reunion.

Cam reluctantly relinquished the contact and moved aside.

"How is she?" he asked anxiously.

"She needs rest. I'm going to give her a sedative. And I want to keep her in the hospital for observation."

After the man had administered the drug, Jo stretched out her hand to Cam. "Don't leave me."

"I won't."

He was still holding her fingers tightly as he felt them relax and saw her eyelids flutter.

"I'm riding in the ambulance with her," he told the doctor.

"She won't know you're there."

"I think she will."

JO AWOKE to ribbons of sunlight filtering through half-closed venetian blinds. She didn't know where she was. For one terrible moment of confusion, the fear was back.

Dig the bolt out of the wall. Get away. Before he takes you to the chapel. She struggled to push herself up. A hand pressed against her shoulder, and she gasped.

"Jo. It's all over. The nightmare is over."

"Cam."

Safety. Freedom. She looked up at him in wonder, still not quite able to believe that they were here together.

"You've been sitting there beside my bed," she said softly.

"Yes."

Eons passed as they stared at each other—taking in details that only lovers see. Transmitting silent messages that only lovers hear.

She was still so pale.

A two-day growth of beard darkened his jaw.

Her eyes were so large and blue.

A lock of dark hair had fallen across his forehead. She reached up to push it back.

"Jo, I've been sitting here, wondering how you were going to feel about me when you woke up."

"Why?"

His voice was raw. "Because if I'd only believed what you were trying to tell me about Collin, none of this would have happened."

"Oh, Cam, that's not true."

He swallowed. "My brother and Art Nugent, the man who kidnapped you, had a—a—relationship. Art was the one who stole the designs from Randolph Electronics."

"I figured that out—from things he said, hints he dropped."

"Did you figure out why he picked you for his next victim? He wanted to get back at me—for not giving him a job in the design department at Randolph."

She found his hand and squeezed it. "No, Cam. Getting back at you was just a dividend. An accident, really. He told me it was a piece of luck for him."

She saw some of the tension go out of Cam's expression and continued, "He kidnapped me because I was the maid of honor in a wedding—like Denise. He was doing the same thing over and over again—repeating his experience with her."

"Denise?"

"He talked a lot about her—about what she meant to him. It's all pretty crazy. But it made some kind of twisted sense to him. It goes back to Collin. I think he really cared for your brother, and he cracked up after he died. He blamed himself for the suicide. It made him want to change his life—to go straight. Right after that, he saw Denise in church and in his disturbed mind, she reminded him of an angel. He thought she could save him—turn his life around. He tried to convince himself he was attracted to her. But she rejected him, and he killed her."

"Oh, my God. He told you all that?"

"Some of it. In bits and pieces. Some I figured out. After that, he kept repeating the experience because he hated her so much and blamed her for his failures."

Cam's voice struggled for even timbre. "Jo, the tapes. The things he said he was going to do to you—"

"Just threats. To make it sound like he wanted a woman. I don't think he could function with a female."

"Jo—I—"

"Cam, stop punishing yourself. It's over. Just hold me, please."

There was no way he could refuse that request. But there were still things he had to say. "Jo, I need you so damn much. I didn't realize how much pain was locked up inside me until I started loving you. But I was still afraid to trust my feelings. It was as if I had to choose either you or Collin. Then when I started to suspect what he'd done to his own company, to my father, I really couldn't handle it."

Jo tightened her arms around him, knowing that it would take time for him to get over the sorrow. But she would be there to help him. "What Collin did doesn't wipe out all the good years when you were growing up. I know it's hard for you now, but you'll see that eventually."

"But he—"

"Probably he was being used—not doing the actual stealing. I think he realized that and couldn't find a way out."

"Yes."

"It's hard to let go of the past—to let yourself see things differently."

"Yes."

"I'm not just talking about you. I'm talking about myself, too." She raised her head so she could meet his eyes. "I was attracted to you the moment we met."

"Attracted to a nutty inventor?"

"Not nutty. Intense. But I was afraid to trust my feelings, too. Abby helped me understand what I was doing. I kept telling myself no one could replace Skip. I was really afraid to take another chance on happiness."

"Jo, I swear I'll make you happy."

"I know you will."

They smiled at each other. Then his lips found hers again for a long, deep kiss, rich with promise for the future.

It was incredible to be held by him again. She felt sheltered. Cherished. Everything she'd been terrified to let herself want.

It was incredible to hold her again. His joy soared. She wanted him. She wasn't blaming him for all the things he'd failed to see and all the things he'd failed to do. Instead she was clinging to him with the same desperation he felt.

"Jo, I love you."

"Oh, Cam, I love you, too. I wanted to tell you that when I made the recording. I knew he wouldn't let me."

"Hearing your voice—knowing he had you..." He couldn't say the rest of it. But he didn't have to. She understood.

All the forces of nature couldn't have separated them as they clung together.

After long moments, she looked up into his eyes, her own twinkling. "I guess this means you've gotten over your aversion to detectives."

"You do have a smart remark for every occasion."

"Yup."

"How would you feel about my putting a certain sassy redheaded private eye on a lifetime retainer?"

For once, Jo O'Malley was speechless.

"Does that mean she'll take the job?"

"You've got a deal."

Harlequin Intrigue®

A SPAULDING & DARIEN MYSTERY
by Robin Francis

An engaging pair of amateur sleuths—Jenny Spaulding and Peter Darien—were introduced to Harlequin Intrigue readers in #147, BUTTON, BUTTON (Oct. 1990). Jenny and Peter will return for further spine-chilling romantic adventures in April 1991 in #159, DOUBLE DARE in which they solve their next puzzling mystery. Two other books featuring Jenny and Peter will follow in the A SPAULDING AND DARIEN MYSTERY series.

IBB-1A

Everyone loves a spring wedding, and this April, Harlequin cordially invites you to read the most romantic wedding book of the year

With This Ring

ONE WEDDING—FOUR LOVE STORIES FROM YOUR FAVORITE HARLEQUIN AUTHORS!

The church is booked, the reception arranged and the invitations mailed. All Diane Bauer and Nick Granatelli have to do is walk down the aisle. Little do they realize that the most cherished day of their lives will spark so many romantic notions....

Available wherever Harlequin books are sold.

You'll flip . . . your pages won't!
Read paperbacks *hands-free* with

Book Mate • I

The perfect "mate" for all your romance paperbacks

**Traveling • Vacationing • At Work • In Bed • Studying
• Cooking • Eating**

Perfect size for all standard paperbacks, this wonderful invention makes reading a pure pleasure! Ingenious design holds paperback books OPEN and FLAT so even wind can't ruffle pages — leaves your hands free to do other things. Reinforced, wipe-clean vinyl-covered holder flexes to let you turn pages without undoing the strap . . . supports paperbacks so well, they have the strength of hardcovers!

Pages turn WITHOUT opening the strap

SEE-THROUGH STRAP

Reinforced back stays flat

Built in bookmark

BOOK MARK

BACK COVER HOLDING STRIP

10" x 7¼", opened.
Snaps closed for easy carrying, too.